the
party
room
GET IT STARTED

Look for the next gripping stories in
The Party Room Trilogy,
by Morgan Burke

AFTER HOURS

LAST CALL

the
party
room
GET IT STARTED

MORGAN BURKE

SIMON PULSE

New York London Toronto Sydney

This book is a work of fiction. Any references to historical events, real people, or real locales are used fictitiously. Other names, characters, places, and incidents are the product of the author's imagination, and any resemblance to actual events or locales or persons, living or dead, is entirely coincidental.

⋀⋀⋀ SIMON PULSE
An imprint of Simon & Schuster
Children's Publishing Division
1230 Avenue of the Americas, New York, NY 10020

SIMON PULSE and colophon are registered trademarks of Simon & Schuster, Inc.

A Parachute Press Book
Designed by Greg Stadnyk
The text of this book was set in Photina.
Manufactured in the United States of America
First Simon Pulse edition February 2005

10 9 8 7 6 5 4 3 2 1

Library of Congress Control Number 2004105412
ISBN 0-689-87225-9

the party room

GET IT STARTED

Part One

Prologue

I've been waiting.

That's right.

Waiting right here all this time.

Watching every move you make.

Searching for the right moment.

Oh, I've been so good.

I've been sooooo UNDER CONTROL!

But I knew it couldn't last for long.

No, it couldn't.

Because I SAW you.

I saw what you DID!

And you have no idea, do you?

No idea what's about to happen next.

What's about to happen to YOU!

It's an art, really.

To be this under cover.

To be sooooo gooooood.

Do you really think you can run wild, just like that?

Do you? DO YOU?

Well, it will all end soon enough, won't it?

Because I'm about to throw a party.

"No, I *didn't* see it," seventeen-year-old Kirsten Sawyer told her friend, Samantha Byrne.

"Come on. Admit it, you looked. I *know* you," Sam said, her hazel eyes sparkling in the dimness of the Party Room as she stood under a sign that said DRINKING AGE 21 and screamed ignore me.

Ignore was what Kirsten desperately wanted to do to Sam right then. It was Friday—a crisp October night and, *hello*, the bar was open. But Sam was her best friend of all time, and Kirsten couldn't ignore her. Well, okay, no one could—friend or foe, male or female. Sam was like a weather front. Whenever she entered the Party Room, the music volume seemed to jack up and the brick walls vibrated. Distracted boyfriends sized up Sam's Scandinavia-perfect cheekbones, shoulder-length platinum hair, Maxim-ready figure, and killer fashion sense. Suddenly every girl was thinking that maybe she should have done more with her makeup or worn that push-up bra—*anything* to offset the pull of Sam's eyes. The eyes that could take a boy's free will and fry it to a crisp.

Even Kirsten would admit that she could fry some wills of her own, with her superlong chestnut-colored hair, America's Next Top Model–length legs, and a smile that had inspired more than a few love poems. Okay, bad ones mostly, but hey, it's high school and what really counts is the thought. Sam and Kirsten were both, after all, part of New York City's exclusive Woodley School in Riverdale—the Bronx really, but don't tell anyone. A group that defined what it meant to be hot and young and rich at the center of the world in the twenty-first century.

Tonight, Kirsten could see that Sam was in a state, with her eye on her used-to-be boyfriend, Brandon Yardley, and her mind set on major-tease mode. Kirsten did not, at that moment, care to focus on the place Sam was eyeing. Not after having spent three grueling hours at a last-minute Kaplan Review class followed by forty-five minutes of coaxing the life back into the two pools of brownish mud formerly known as her eyes. "Okay . . . yeah," Kirsten said, humoring her. "You're right, Spammie, it's a sock. I mean, it's definitely not real."

"Wait. It's moving!" Sam's eyes were as wide as softballs. "Kirsten, it's alive!"

That did it. Now Kirsten *had* to look, couldn't *help* looking. Brandon Alexander Yardley, slouched against the bar with his unlit cigarette and strong jaw and the faded outline down the front of his jeans that obviously did wonders for his self-esteem. Yes, it *did* look like there was some extra-enhancement in there, but no, it *wasn't* moving.

Just the idea that she was checking it out forced Kirsten to release an involuntary giggle, which wasn't exactly a stellar move. Because here on the Upper East Side of Manhattan, where the value of your seven-figure apartment matched the size of your trust fund, where *everyone* who was *anyone* had already seen *everything* that meant anything (or so they say), getting embarrassed

3

over ogling a guy's, um, *equipment* was far from cool.

Like right now. Like when the subject of your ogle ogled back . . . with great manly pride. "Hey babe, you like what you see?" Brandon called out, thrusting his hips forward a little.

"Oh, please," Kirsten said, trying to sound unaffected and unembarrassed. "I didn't bring my microscope. So why don't you turn your sorry-ass piece of false advertising back toward the bar, where it belongs."

And wonder of wonders, Brandon's never-before-seen modesty burst from hiding and, face turning red, he did as he was told.

Sam let out a whoop. "You go, girl! I didn't know you had it in you."

Kirsten shrugged. She wasn't normally quick with the comebacks the way Sam was, but this time was different. "Brandon puts to rest any doubts that the human race was descended from barbaric, apelike beings," she said.

"That's why we're celebrating my Liberation from Brandon Day, right?" Sam nodded and slung her arm around Kirsten's shoulders and led her to the dance floor.

"Right," Kirsten said, looking around to see who was there tonight.

Kirsten spotted the short and sassy blond haircut of her other best friend, Julie Pembroke. She floated by in her usual neck-to-toe black, with a tight knit shirt that accented her best assets, and of course had drawn a following of five guys in various stages of drool control. "Sorry-ass piece of false advertising?" Julie said. "I've got to remember that one."

"Hi, Kirsten!" shouted Sarah Goldstein, the Cheerleader with the Heart of Chocolate who could spend a week on one food group—sweets—and still look as if she could work a runway. She, as always, was entertaining her own Circle of Male Life, and teasing them with a flip of her wavy auburn locks.

Kirsten waved to her, and to Carla Hernandez, a.k.a. Carla the Geek, who disproved the conventional wisdom that a person who understood I.T. could not be H.O.T. Carla's skirt flared as she danced, revealing a body more lethal than an attachment with executable malicious code, whatever that meant.

As Kirsten moved to the beat, she felt her

cares flying away. She had been *dying* to dance. "What did you see in Brandon, anyway?" she asked Sam. "I mean, aside from the fact that he's hot."

"Well, first of all," Sam replied, "what you said about the microscope—it isn't true."

"Really?" Kirsten asked, glancing back at him.

"Tape measure, sister-girl," Sam said with a slow, sly grin. "Or . . . barometer? Isn't that what measures *pressure?*"

Kirsten grinned. "You are so, *so* bad."

Sam threw back her head and laughed, long and deep. "Well, okay . . . seriously? I loved the way he got mad when I called him Brandy Alexander, for one thing. When he's not drunk or stoned or depressed or pissed off, he can be funny and fun to be with. Sexy, too. And—don't faint—*once* . . . I think it was August ninth at three forty-seven . . . he was actually kind. I mean it. Not that you'd want to spend your life with him. He's great for someone with a short attention span like me. The problem is Woodley. The more boyfriends you ditch, the harder it is to avoid them all."

It was true. Woodley was a small place.

And not exactly modest. Depending on the newspaper you read, it was "the A-list alma mater of movie stars, heiresses, and a good chunk of the Ivy League" or "a Depraved Preppy Sex Den," but frankly, Woodley girls were much more likely to make the Style section than the gossip column.

On a Friday like this, with the school week over and the night young and the East River breeze wafting past the open doors of the Upper East Side bars, people knew you went to Woodley. It was kind of funny, really. The shopkeepers beckoned you inside, eyes on your well-stocked Prada handbag. The salivating boys shouted from BMWs with New Jersey MD plates or MY SON IS A GREAT NECK NORTH HONOR ROLL STUDENT bumper stickers. Last month's rap hits blared from the speakers. As for the public-high-school crowd, well, let's not go there.

They all knew who you were.

And you just. Didn't. Care.

You headed to the Party Room, where your friends were waiting, the bartender was pouring, and the world was perfect.

"His masculinity threatened, the brooding

priapic young Brandon pretends his ex-girlfriend does not exist," said Sam in her best news-anchor voice as Kirsten swam her way through the crowd, pulling Sam toward the bar.

Kirsten looked over her shoulder. "Priapic?"

"Definition at eleven," Sam replied. "Fortunately, tonight Sam is sniffing out a real man, not a Goat Boy with a five o'clock shadow who reminds her of her new step-father, the dreaded Rolf from Düsseldorf."

"Uh, Rolf doesn't *have* a five o'clock shadow," she reminded Sam.

"Exactly." Sam sat at the bar, waving toward Scott, the bartender. "I have a new policy: No hooking up with high-school boys who look older than Mom's husband. Rolf still gets *carded*, Kirsten—plus, he speaks *German.* What do they *talk* about? What do they have in common? I mean, one minute they're pumping iron at the gym together, the next minute they're pumping each other."

"Uh . . . ew!" Kirsten said, trying to fight off the mental image of Sam's mom, Bobbi Byrne, doing it with her German trainer. Then she flashed a sudden Whitening Strip smile at

Scott the bartender, who had finally turned her way. He was an early Tom-Cruise-by-way-of-Justin-Timberlake-with-an-extra-dose-of-testosterone type, perfect eye candy when the dance floor was not enough. And a really nice guy too. "I'd like the usual," she said, winking. "A Shirley Temple."

"The same for me, Scotty," Sam said.

Scott smiled that crooked, sexy little half-smile, which, if he could somehow make it transferable to other guys, would make him a fortune in licensing deals and a lot of girls very happy. He was also famous for having the fastest hands on the East Side, and in moments two martini glasses filled with fresh pinkish-amber drinks appeared on the bar top.

"To freedom," Sam said, holding up her drink, careful not to spill.

Kirsten clinked her glass with Sam's and downed her drink. Definitely not a Shirley Temple. She ordered another one. "No worries!" she said, taking a sip.

"Good. Because we're young, gorgeous, *and single!*" Drink high in the air, hips moving, Sam danced her way onto the floor. "Come on, Kissyface. Let's go shake our tail feathers!"

Sam was the only person in the world allowed to call Kirsten "Kissyface." And if anyone aside from Kirsten called Sam "Spammie," she'd better hold on to her self-esteem for dear life.

The throbbing pulse of an old-school Jay Z track began to take over the room. Kirsten was feeling so great, she kicked off her Manolos, which were killing her, and cut loose with her friends.

Sam's white-blond hair was flying all over the place, catching the light and drawing attention to her antique silver earrings, shaped like slender, delicate, hanging grapes. Kirsten loved those earrings—along with Sam's matching bracelet, both one-of-a-kind gifts from her grandmother that Sam hardly ever took off. She smiled at Kirsten, then reached into the pocket of her D&G jeans and held out a tiny white pill.

"Want to share?" Sam asked. "Brandon gave it to me last week, but that was before I dumped him. I don't think I'll be getting anything like this again."

Kirsten hesitated. She was kind of gone already. *Oh, why not?* she thought. *It's a cele-*

bration! She took the pill from Sam, turned, and bit it in half before swallowing.

Soon her Kaplan class faded into memory, lost in a blur of arms, torsos, legs—sometimes Sam . . . sometimes others . . . the usual Woodley crowd . . . also Leslie Fenk, blond and irresistible in a Scarlett-Johannsen-meets-Julia-Stiles way, known as the Woodley Bitch by the boys (and girls) she had seduced and dropped . . . and there in the corner, in his last year at Woodley before taking his drop-dead gorgeous butt to Princeton, was Gabe Garson, a.k.a. Gay Gabe, who was dancing with Emma "Get a Life" Lewis.

Uh-oh, Kirsten thought. It was only a matter of time before Emma saw them. The girl had some kind of weird Sam radar. *Four . . . three . . . two . . .*

Julie spun away from the three guys she was dancing with to give Sam a warning. "Orange Alert," she said, just as Kirsten saw Emma's eyes light up.

The Woodley junior with the mousy brown hair waved at them, then started to dance her way over, her moves totally mimicking Sam's. Poor dull Emma idolized Sam, which in itself

11

wasn't *so* unusual, but the girl, unfortunately, was a little like a hangover: She came on hard and lingered way too long.

Sam groaned. "Oh, God. You've got to get me *away* from her."

Kirsten laughed. "Come on. She's annoying, yes, but all in all she's pretty harmless."

"Kind of like the plague," Julie added with a grin.

Sam shook her head. "You guys wouldn't think it was so funny if you were the one she was obsessed with. I mean, she copies everything I do. One day she's going to make all of you into her best friends, then bump me off so she can take over my life."

"What's up, homey?" Emma chirped, which was something Sam used to say a lot, like a decade ago.

"Ahhh-chooo!" Sam pretended to sneeze. "I'm fine. Just at the beginning stages of a highly contagious deadly flu."

"We're already infected," Julie said, "but you still have a chance." With that, she pulled Sam away before Emma could leach on to them for the night.

Kirsten gave Emma a weak smile and a

shrug, then followed her friends to the other side of the dance floor. Sweeping past a table, she put down her drink and really started to move to the beat of the awesome song blaring over the bar's sound system. She felt her body take flight. Hips, elbows, shoulders—going on their own power.

Soon the dance floor was clearing.

"Showtime!" Sam shouted.

It was just Kirsten and Sam and Julie now. The rest circled around, watching. Shouting. Cheering. Kirsten caught glances. Guy-glances. They wanted her . . . maybe . . . which was cool, totally cool—but at the moment, she didn't care. All that mattered was the motion and the music and her friends . . . her friends for all time . . .

Click.

A flash went off to Kirsten's right. Near the bar.

Click.

Kirsten looked over, expecting to see the Style Section guy from the *New York Times* or the greasy pervert from the tabloids. But it wasn't either.

It was Brandon.

"Take *this* . . . ," Sam said, pulling up her shirt and showing a nanosecond of breast.

Click.

Too late.

Click. Click.

Now Brandon was dancing with them, bouncing to an unidentified beat, wobbling and breathing heavily. Kirsten made a mental note to be grateful she didn't have to smell that breath. He circled around Sam, leaning close to her face, zeroing in on different parts of her body with his camera.

Click!

Sam leaped back, making it look like part of the choreography, and Kirsten stepped between them. "Enough, Brandon," she said.

"Hmm-MMMMmmm," sang Sam, the *I-am-OUT-of-here* tune that she and Kirsten had used since All-Souls preschool. Then, showing the form made famous in Madame Baudry's fourth-grade ballet class, Sam *chasséd* across the floor—away from Brandon.

Kirsten followed, but she couldn't match Brandon's experience running through a backfield of prep school gridiron kings. "Yo!" he shouted, lurching through the crowd (or maybe he was dancing). "Where you going?"

"As far away from you as I can," Sam called back. "You photographed me on my bad side."

"Come *on*," Brandon mumbled, his voice slurred and a notch too loud. "You know you want me. Admit it."

"You're right, Brandy Alexander, oh . . . *oh . . . OH*, I soooo want you . . . ," she said breathlessly, "*. . . to go away!*"

"Don't be a tease, Sam. You know I don't like it." Brandon grabbed Sam's arm, but she shook him off and ran.

"Kirsten!" she cried out, heading for the door.

Brandon sprinted after her.

Kirsten tried to follow. But the Party Room was full of gawkers, and the crowd closed in. *"Out of my way!"* she called out, elbowing through.

She heard a scream. A slam. A chair falling and skittering across the room.

And then Sam's voice.

"Let me go!" she cried. "Stop it! *Help! Somebody help me! He's hurting me!*"

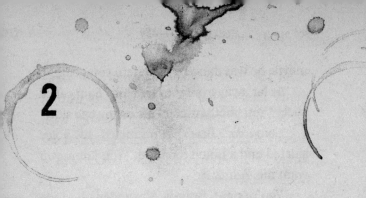

2

Kirsten grabbed Brandon by the shirt collar. Julie, racing over with her entourage close behind, got the waistband. They both yanked hard.

He was a big guy, but he was drunk and stoned and he stumbled backward, his thick hands letting go of Sam's arms. She fell against the door while Brandon thrashed about, finally tripping on his own feet and tumbling to the floor.

The worst part was, no one was helping. No one was doing a goddamn thing!

"What's going on here?" Scott the Bartender said, pushing people aside.

Kirsten and Julie rushed to Sam and helped her up. "Are you okay?" Kirsten asked.

"Never been better," Sam said loudly and angrily, brushing off her clothes. "You know, I

think the floor is, like, mahogany or something? That's what we did our floors with at
home. Isn't that *interesting?* Being with
Brandy Alexander is so educational. You see
things you never would have seen with a
human boyfriend."

"You're such a bitch!" Brandon said, stag-
gering to his feet.

Sam opened her mouth, and then closed it.
If Kirsten didn't know better, she'd have
thought Sam was kind of upset by Brandon's
not-so-original remark, which was weird
because it certainly wasn't the first time Sam
had been called a bitch.

Scott pulled him up the rest of the way.
"Out of here, Yardley. Go home, sleep it off,
and explain it to your mom and dad in the
morning."

"I'm not going anywhere." Brandon stag-
gered back a couple of steps, pointing a finger
at Sam. "Nobody makes an ass out of me and
gets away with it. I'm going to get you back,
Sam. . . . I'm going to be your worst night-
muh-muh . . ." Brandon could hardly stand
up now. He barreled to the front door. The
crowd parted like the Red Sea to let him out.

Scott handed Sam some napkins from the bar. "Are you okay? Do you want me to call you a cab?"

"I didn't know you cared." Sam smiled. "No, seriously, I'm okay."

"Brandon isn't," said Josh Bergen, a senior from Talcott Prep who had been part of Julie's inner dancing circle. "Five bucks says he's facedown in some Upper East Side Shitzu dog doo. Any takers? Let's go have a look, shall we?"

Talcott was Woodley's rival school, and Josh definitely had a Talcott sense of humor.

"That's disgusting," Kirsten said, walking Sam back toward the tables with Julie. The music had changed to a slow, sexy Ashanti song, and the crowd was beginning to dance again.

As Kirsten and Sam sat at a table in the corner, Julie headed to the bar for drinks.

"I can't believe he did that," Sam said. "I can't believe he *attacked* me. Look at my hands—they're shaking."

Kirsten took hold of her friend's hands and tried to calm her down. "He's a creep, Sam. I always thought so, but I just never admitted it to you. I guess I should have."

"No. This is partly my fault, Kirsten. My big mouth. It's like, I'm off him but there's still a connection. Why can't I just break up like a normal person?"

"Um, give me a minute, let me guess. Maybe because *he's* . . . a pig?" Kirsten replied.

"But that's the thing. He isn't. Not really. I mean, I *did* choose to go out with him, right? He's only like this at parties when he gets high." Sam picked out the cashews from the snack dish on the table. "See, I think Brandon does drugs because he's insecure about being a country boy. He grew up in Iowa. Idaho. Ohio. One of the O states. You know what his favorite hobby is? Duck hunting. With his dad."

"You're kidding me, right?" Kirsten asked.

Sam nodded and smiled, twirling the ends of her hair with a finger. The girls were both quiet for a moment, and Sam looked as if her mind were a million miles away.

"What are you thinking about?" Kirsten asked, even though she knew the answer.

"What else?" Sam shrugged. "You know, I try to be all tough and make fun of Brandon, but . . . I really liked him, Kirsten. I did. It was just too intense—what he was getting into was—"

"Getting into?" Kirsten said. "Meaning the drugs? Was he going hard-core or something?"

The question went unanswered. Sam dipped her hand into a bowl of cashews on the table, lost in some thought and staring vaguely in the direction of the bar, where Julie was picking up three delicious-looking pinkish drinks.

Then, suddenly, Sam smacked the table. "Forget it. I'm glad I dumped him. A person has to break from the past, Kirsten. If you do the same things all the time, your brain gets all, like, spongiform. Right?"

"Uh, right."

Spongiform? Kirsten made a mental note to look that one up, too.

"Screw the same-old, same-old!" Sam stood up from the table and shouted out loud: "*Screw* the same conversations and the same gossip—and the Upper East Side and the Junior League and the Ivy League—and Mom's Nazi husband. I'm sick of my life! *I want to do something wild and unexpected!*"

She pulled open a button on her blouse. And she leaped across the dance floor, landing somewhere between a bump and a grind, and dancing like this was the last day of her life.

Julie came back with three drinks and set them on the table. "Who plugged her in?"

"You know . . . it happens every few weeks, whenever she breaks up with a guy," Kirsten said.

"Soon, there aren't going to be any guys left for her," Julie said, sitting down. "I give my boys at least three weeks. Then the flush."

Kirsten smiled. Under the tight sweaters and do-it-to-me-now shoes, there was a shy girl in there *somewhere.* Yeah, right. "I don't know, Jules. I think this one's really hard for her. It hasn't been easy breaking away."

"Oh? Are you sure?" Julie was looking out to the dance floor, her eyebrows raised.

A new guy, someone Kirsten had never seen before, was dancing with Sam. A hottie wearing vintage worn Levi's and a classic Phish T-shirt. He was tall, had scruffy red hair, and a chiseled rugged face. And he seemed a little older, like maybe he'd wandered into the wrong bar or something. A junior or senior in college, Kirsten figured. This Phish shirt was odd because he was more than a little dangerous looking. . . .

And totally Sam's type.

Here we go again, Kirsten thought, taking a sip of her drink. Mmm . . . a pomegranate martini. Just what the doctor ordered. "Who's the Viking?" she asked Julie.

"Never seen him before," Julie replied.

"Well, she's found hers. I guess it's time we found ours." Kirsten threw back half her drink. "Come on, let's dance and look irresistible."

The floor was body-to-body now. As Kirsten made her way across the room, she could see Sam was weaving among the hordes, her new guy following her like Erik the Red charting a course to the New World.

The Party Room was hot tonight.

Really hot.

Kirsten tossed her head back and drank it all in. *Same-old same-old?* Nah. She loved this place. On the Upper East Side, where a hundred brushed-steel Euro trash and décor-of-the-month clubs lined First and Second

Avenues, full of suburban kids seeking other suburban kids, the Party Room was something from another time. Just an old brick building with no name, no markings, no window—as if the last guy who lived there put on his hobnail boots and left two hundred years ago, and the house was still waiting for him.

A historical plaque near the corner said it was a stop on the Underground Railroad or something, but if not for that you'd never look twice, never think of entering—unless you *knew.* Because when you went down the creaky stairs and stepped through the thick oak door, warped by its own weight and age, you entered a kind of Alice in Wonderland world that was neither basement nor ground floor, a world of brick walls and recessed lighting, polished oak bar and plasma TV screen, floors worn smooth by centuries of foot traffic, and monster speakers whose sound somehow barely filtered up to the street—and you knew you were part of a secret, an address passed from class to class, hardly ever straying from the Woodley fold.

And judging from the fact that the management never spent a penny on advertising, they must have liked it that way too. The Party Room was forever old, forever new. And always hot, hot, hot.

Scott, she noticed, was no longer at the bar. She glanced around and saw him talking to a cop in the open front door. Once in a while the neighbors would call in complaints. Loitering, trash talking, kids peeing against the building walls. Like it was such a *shock* to New Yorkers that a place called the Party Room actually had parties? Hello?

The officer didn't seem to care. Dozens of kids, mostly Woodley students, passed him by, shouting, laughing at the top of their lungs, many of them saying hi to Sam as she made her way toward the door with Erik the Red.

"That was a fast recovery from heartbreak," Julie said, dancing with Kirsten and Gay Gabe. "I think it might even be a record."

"She's got good taste," Gabe said, practically drooling over Sam's new guy.

Sam let out a tuneless blast of singing. Normally she had a great voice, which meant only one thing. "She's all done," Kirsten said.

"Kisssyyyyyfaaace!" Sam called out from the door. "Don't leave without me!" She put her right hand to her ear, thumb and pinkie extended, and mouthed, *I'll call you.*

Kirsten took her cell phone from her pocket, flipped it open, and looked at the time.

12:09 A.M.

She changed her ringer setting to High and waved good-bye to her friend.

3

"So long, farewell, *au revoir!*" Julie sang out.

"You're wasted . . . ," Kirsten sang back, "and also very flaaaaaaat."

"Wasted, yeah." Julie straightened up. Her size 36Ds smartly saluted the sleeping denizens of Park Avenue. "But flat? I don't think so."

"Can you make it home by yourself?" Kirsten asked.

"My girls will point the way." She turned her breasts up East Eighty-fourth Street. Yodeling, she wove her way home on the rain-slicked pavement. "God, Kirsten, all these houses look the same, don't they?"

Kirsten waited until Julie let herself into the cozy confines of her brownstone town house—the correct one—then closed her jacket tight and turned to walk home.

Scott's martinis were still whirling through her system, too, and her feet slipped and slid off the heels of her fabulous Manolos. She thought about hailing a cab, but the cool night air felt good against her face, especially after the muggy closeness of the Party Room. Besides, it was starting to drizzle and you could never get a cab on the East Side in any sort of precipitation whatsoever. Especially if you needed one. It was some kind of municipal law.

Her footsteps clattered on the sidewalk as she headed toward Park Avenue. She felt like that actor in the old movie *Some Like It Hot*. The one who dressed as a woman but couldn't handle heels. Jack Lemmon. That was his name.

The walk was short, and so familiar, she could do it in her sleep. Left on Park, three blocks downtown to East Eighty-first, then right to Fifth Avenue. Her apartment building was on the corner. Across the street from the Metropolitan Museum of Art and familiar to the world from the hundreds of movies filmed in front of her building. Hector would be on front-door duty tonight. He was the nicest doorman ever, as opposed to the creepy night guy in Sam's building.

Sam.

Where *was* she?

Kirsten stopped walking and pulled out her cell and checked it for the fourth time since Sam had left the Party Room.

Voice mail . . . nothing.

Missed calls . . . nothing.

Received calls . . . her own phone number, three times. The times Mom had called to screech.

The phone's screen said 2:41 A.M.

Kirsten sighed. *Don't leave without* me, she remembered. That's what Sam had said. Right, Kirsten had heard that one before. But Sam also said she'd call. And lately she was pretty good about that. By now, she usually checked in.

But Sam had lost track of time.

The last time this happened was a total disaster, the night Sam had ended up in a Vassar dorm room passed out on the floor with four college guys and an unopened magnum of Dom Pérignon. She attempted to sneak it out at 4:00 in the morning only to catch her heel on the doorjamb and smash the bottle to bits in the hallway.

That was the night Kirsten tried to set a limit: 2:00 A.M. for cell-phone-check-in time. Which was kind of dumb, like something a parent would do, so of course she didn't push it.

Still, Kirsten was pissed. Mainly, she had to admit, because she wanted details about Erik the Red.

Kirsten turned around, deciding to take the long way—back over to Lexington, around to East Eighty-third. There, she would pass the brownstone of Ambassador Reynault, whose Yale-sophomore son, Julian, had been Sam's summer fling. Maybe Sam had ended up there tonight. If so, the light would be on in the basement room, affectionately known as Julian's Den of Delights.

But 141 East Eighty-third was dark, top to bottom, like every other brownstone on the block. Everyone asleep in the middle of the City That Never Sleeps.

As she passed Number 127, she heard footsteps behind her.

Clup . . . clup . . . clup . . . clup . . .

She turned quickly. The way she'd been

trained. The instinct every New York girl cultivated. The idea was to face the person, meet him eye to eye. If it's just a nobody, he won't care. If it's an attacker, you'll catch him off-guard, show him you're a person with a will of your own—and he's more likely to back off.

But there were no eyes to meet. Three doors down, a figure slipped into the shadow of a basement entrance.

"Hello?" Kirsten called out.

Nothing.

Kirsten's heart thumped harder in her chest. *Stop being paranoid*, she told herself. *Stop messing with your own head. You're almost home.*

A set of headlights appeared, two blocks away, but the car turned down Lex, leaving the whole street empty down to the river. Definitely, at this point, a cab was the best idea. Maybe she'd have better luck with them on Park. She turned and began walking fast.

Clup, clup, clup, clup . . .

Shit, Kirsten thought.

She crossed the street, and the footsteps crossed too.

She stopped, and they stopped.

Screw the mind games. Focus, Kirsten. Straight line. Park Avenue ahead.

Her ankle twisted in her shoes, and she leaned down to slip them off without breaking stride, but the right one was stuck and she smacked against a scrawny maple, turning around in time to see a pair of shoulders, a coat, legs running toward her, and she didn't want to look, didn't want to attempt the eye contact thing because she was scared now and she *needed a cab!* And so she stopped thinking altogether and ran, ran full speed, barefoot, clinging to the shoes and watching the amber lights of Park Avenue coming closer, the cabs gliding past the center median, uptown, downtown . . .

Clup-clup-clup-clup . . .

"TAXI!" Racing onto Park, she shot into the intersection too fast and too scared to notice the livery cab screaming toward her, uptown, trying to beat a yellow light.

SKREEEEEEEE . . .

Kirsten jumped into the street, toward the median, and the car barreled by her, careening through the light, barely missing the line of parked cars on the other side of the street, and Kirsten kept running, across the intersection, left on Park, ignoring the stream of Spanish curse words that spewed from the cab and thrusting her arm out like a crazed bird hoping to flag a real cab, going her way, but there was nothing, *nothing,* as if the drivers had planned to shun her on purpose.

She veered west on East Eighty-second Street—familiar territory, high brownstone stoops—and ducked into the sunken area behind the steps leading to a basement rental apartment. In the sudden stillness, her violent heartbeats felt like fists to her chest. She crouched down in the shadows and willed herself quiet, listening for footsteps.

A truck rumbled up Madison. A horn blared on Park. But East Eighty-second was silent, as silent as New York could be.

He was gone. She could make it home by herself. Lesson learned. No harm done.

Stand. Breathe. Move.

Kirsten stepped out from the stoop and onto the sidewalk. She looked left and right and began to walk, peering carefully into the slanted shadows of the rising stoops.

Three blocks to home.

At the corner of Madison Avenue, she turned left—

And felt a hand grab her by the arm.

"Noooooo!" Kirsten screamed, kicked, and fought with all her might.

"Ahhh! Ow! Stop it!"

The hand let go.

Brandon Yardley stumbled away. "Jesus, what is *wrong* with you?"

"Oh, my God." Kirsten was hyperventilating. She couldn't see straight. "You asshole."

"Holy shit, Kirsten, that hurt," he said, rubbing his leg. "And what the hell are you screaming about?"

"That *hurt?*" Kirsten spun around on her bare feet and walked down Madison. "You follow me like a pervert, you make me run into the street where I almost get killed, then you attack me. *Now take a wild guess what I'm screaming about!*"

Brandon walked with her, and Kirsten could smell the beer on his breath.

"I wasn't following you," he said. "I just saw you come around the corner. I wanted to ask where Sam was. That's all."

"Sam?" Kirsten turned to face him. "What do you want with her?"

"We have some unfinished business," he said, staring at her with a kind of desperation in his bloodshot eyes. "It's personal."

"Look, Brandon. I don't know where she is," Kirsten began.

"Fine. If you don't want to tell me where my girlfriend is, I'll find her on my own." Brandon turned to leave, but Kirsten stopped him. Clearly the guy was losing his grip on reality and she had to put him in check.

"Brandon," she said slowly, "Sam *isn't* your girlfriend. She doesn't want to see you anymore."

Brandon shrugged as if it were no big deal. "It was just a fight," he said. "She'll be back."

Kirsten shook her head. "Uh, I don't think so," she said. "Her mind is made up. She's already moved on with someone else."

Brandon furrowed his brows. "I saw them," he said through gritted teeth. "I'm going to beat the crap out of that guy just as soon as I find them!"

Kirsten rolled her eyes. She didn't care what Sam had said earlier. Brandon *was* a pig.

A Neanderthal. Plain and simple. "Whatever. You do what you want," she said, "but the party is over. I suggest you get a life!"

Brandon gripped Kirsten's arm tightly, surprising her. His face had turned bright red; the veins in his neck and forehead bulged. "She can't treat me this way. And you can't, either, Kirsten. You tell Sam that. You tell her *nobody* screws Brandon Yardley."

Kirsten yanked her arm away. She was so done. "Yeah. Least of all Sam Byrne," she said, and walked down Eighty-first Street, onto Fifth Avenue, halfway down the block and through the front door of her building with her shoes in her hands.

Hector, the doorman, bolted to his feet. "Kirsten? Are you okay? Your shoes . . ."

Kirsten ran to the elevators, which were out of sight from the street. "I'm fine, Hector. Thanks!"

The elevator opened. Kirsten stepped in, sank to the carpeted floor, closed her eyes, and rode upward. The doors opened right into the front hall of her penthouse apartment, which was dark. Good. That meant Mom and Dad had gone to bed.

Kirsten padded into the dark living room, flicked on a light, and sunk into the goose-down sofa. She inspected her throbbing arm. She was starting to get a bruise where Brandon had grabbed her. Great.

Why do you even bother, Kirsten? she wondered. *You should know better than to get involved with one of Sam's heartbroken beasts.* She glanced at her arm again. *Look where it gets you.*

She stared out the bay window at the darkened museum across the street, at the string of streetlamps snaking into the park toward the Reservoir, and sighed. Somewhere out there Sam was with a cute guy, in some state of substance abuse and/or undress, most likely having the time of her life.

And where was Kirsten?

Kirsten was alone in her apartment, having been chased down and threatened by her best friend's latest castaway. "Wait till I get my hands on you, Sam," she said softly. "You are *so* dead."

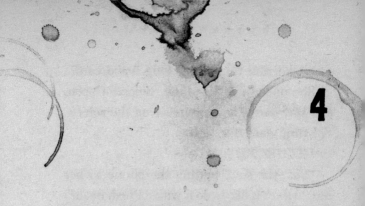

4

The vibration in her pocket awoke Kirsten the next morning.

In her dream she had been running through the neighborhood streets, but instead of Brandon chasing her it was rats, big disgusting sooty subway rats—the animals she hated worst in the world—

DZZZZZZZZ.

She screamed and sat up with a start, fumbling for her cell phone. *That's* what the vibration was.

Her four-poster bed came into focus. She was still dressed in her clothes from last night. On the wall, Ashton Kutscher smiled his customary Good Morning to her. And she felt as if someone had peeled open her head and dropped in broken glass. This was going to be one gigantic hangover. How had she gotten from the sofa to her bed? Was last night—the whole horrible thing—one long, bad dream?

She pulled out the phone, flipped it open, and saw Sam's home number on the screen. The time was 10:42 A.M.

DZZZZZZZZZ.

"So," she said, putting the phone to her ear, "what's it like to do it with a Phish head?"

There was a pause at the other end. "Hello? Is this Kirsten?" Bobbi Byrne asked.

Shit. It was Sam's *mom!* Open mouth, insert filthy, New York City–grime-encrusted foot. "Oh! Hi, Bobbi! What I meant was—"

"It *is* you, thank goodness!" Sam's mom said. "Kirsten, would you tell Sam I need to speak to her right away?"

"Sam?" Kirsten repeated.

"Yes, Kirsten. I've been trying her and you all morning. Last night Sam mentioned that she might be sleeping at your house. Would you please put her on the phone?"

Kirsten took a deep breath.

This was bad form for Sam. Really breaking the Code, which was—more or less—(1) Always complain, always explain (2) Keep in touch (3) When in doubt, cover your girlfriend's butt.

The problem was, you couldn't do (3) very well if you didn't do (2). And you couldn't do any of it well with a raging hangover.

"Well, um . . . ," Kirsten said, "as a matter of fact . . . I can't put Sam on right now. . . ."

"Oh . . . I see," Bobbi said. "I suppose she's with the Fish boy?"

"F-Fish boy?" Kirsten said.

"Kirsten, darling, I heard what you said. Fish Head. I wasn't born yesterday. That must be Spencer Fish's nickname, right? The boy in Model Congress? Is that who she's with?"

Image assault.

The thought of Sam Byrne with helmet-haired Spencer Fish, whose nose looked like a pork roast and whose wardrobe was last updated in 1997, nearly made Kirsten fall off the bed.

In the background she heard a groggy male voice saying, *"Do ve need to call nine-von-von?"*

Rolf from Düsseldorf. With his Teutonic sense of the world, which, if Kirsten didn't handle this situation right, would curdle in a minute. From the way Sam described him, Rolf *would* be the type to call the cops. And

that would be a catastrophe of Olympic pro-
portions. Every sweaty, pencil-chomping,
taped-together-eyeglasses reporter in New
York City was salivating at the chance to find
dirt on a New York Society girl. "Woodley
Coed Home After a Two-Day Bender"—*that's*
what Rolf's meddling would lead to, because
at the moment Sam was probably passed out
on the floor of some friend of a friend of a
friend in Brooklyn Heights or Scarsdale and
wouldn't be awake until half-past lunch. Only
there was *no way* Kirsten would tell that to
Bobbi and Rolf.

"I meant—she's not with me because
she . . . got up early and left," Kirsten said.

"So she's not with the Fish boy?" Bobbi
asked.

"I don't think so," Kirsten said. "She's
probably on her way home right now . . . or
maybe she stopped to get some breakfast or
something. Her cell phone is dead, that's probably why she hasn't called you," she continued. She was on a roll. Sam and Julie would be
proud.

"Oh," Bobbi said. "Okay."

"Don't worry," Kirsten added. "I'm sure

she'll be home any minute . . . if not sooner."

"Thanks, Kirsten," Bobbi said. "I wish all her friends were like you."

Oh, they are, Kirsten wanted to say. *They've been covering for her for years.* "No problem. Talk to you soon. Bye!" She hung up, sank back on the bed, and tapped out Sam's number. Oh, the girl was going to owe her big for this. Maybe brunch at the Plaza—that sounded nice.

"Hello, um, yeah. Sam here. Go ahead and talk, but make it fast. And if you can't make it fast, make it funny. . . ."

At the beep, Kirsten said, "I won't be fast or funny. Where are you? I just got off the phone with your mom, and my nose grew six inches. She thinks you're doing it with Spencer Fish. I told her I'd buy him condoms because it never occurred to him he'd need any. Ha-ha. Just kidding. About some of it. How was Erik the Red? Details, you owe me details. You owe me a lot more, but we'll talk later. Call your mom ASAP, she's getting on my nerves. Good night."

Kirsten hung up and tried to get comfortable on her bed, but the urge to sleep had

41

passed. Her brain still felt like it was in a bowl of broken glass.

A shower was called for. Head function in the morning simply did not begin without something minty and expensive on one's face. Kirsten stood up, slowly. She peeled off her clothes, put on her robe. Then she inched her way into the hall toward the bathroom, one foot at a time.

From Mom and Dad's bedroom at the other end of the apartment she heard a rustling of bedsheets, a snore or two. They'd be good for another hour. She flicked on the bathroom light, then flicked it off. Too bright. Everything was too bright. The night-light would do just fine.

As she closed the bathroom door behind her, she spotted a blinking light on the answering machine in the front hall, by the elevator.

Had that message been there when she'd arrived home? No. It must have come in sometime after 3:00 A.M. or so. But Sam wouldn't call her *house* phone. She always used the cell.

Still, Kirsten tiptoed out of the bathroom and into the front hall. The answering machine sat on an antique table, flashing a "1" in Mailbox 3. *Kirsten's* mailbox.

She pressed Play.

CHHHH . . . SSHHHHH . . . WRONNNN . . .

Great. It was static, the kind of loud and scratchy, obnoxious noise of a cell phone turned on by mistake in someone's pocket. In the background were a car horn and some distant, garbled voices.

Whoever had done this must have had Kirsten's number on speed dial. Kirsten knew that routine—she had all her friends on speed dial. If she didn't lock her phone, and she hit, say, the number 3 inadvertently, she'd send Julie sixty seconds of pocket noise.

She knelt and cocked her ear closer to the machine. Someone was yelling or laughing, it was hard to tell which and impossible to recognize the voice, which was obliterated by the roar of a passing bus and the screech of a car's tires. When that noise died down, Kirsten heard footsteps and the fragment of a conversation.

". . . is this place . . ." were the only words she heard clearly. They could have been from Sam, but it was hard to tell. She turned up the

43

sound and heard the voices continue. One voice was female, that was for sure. The other voice was too hard to tell, too quiet.

". . . doesn't make sense . . ." Yeah, that was Sam, she was fairly sure. There was something about the rhythm. She seemed aggravated about something. *Not aggravated enough to make a real call to her best friend,* Kirsten noted.

The footsteps were quickening now. The voices had stopped, and so had most of the traffic noise. Kirsten heard a thump and a kind of strangled gasp.

And then, piercing through the speaker, clear and sharp, was the knife-edge sound of a scream.

"No . . . NO . . . NO-O-O-O-O-O!"

Kirsten jumped back, and the tape abruptly ended.

It *was* Sam. There was no mistaking the voice.

What had happened? Who was she with? *WHERE WAS SHE?*

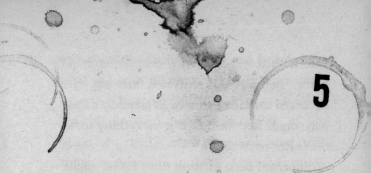

5

"And then I erased it,"

Kirsten said on Monday morning. "I was so freaked out, I pressed the wrong button and I erased the entire message! I can't believe I'm such an idiot!"

"Wait. You *heard* Sam scream?" Carla Hernandez asked. She was sitting next to Kirsten at a lab table in Mr. Costas's third-period biology class. "Or you *thought* you heard her scream? Maybe it wasn't her."

Sarah, Julie, and Leslie pulled up their stools around Kirsten in a circle. Today's experiment was the dissection of a fetal pig, which had been pinned to a lab tray on its side and was at the moment totally ignored by the group except for Leslie, who let out a little "Ew . . ." before pulling her stool the farthest away.

"I'm *sure* it was her," Kirsten said. Gazing down at the bio specimen, she felt her eyes blur with tears. Normally, dissections didn't bother her, but this shriveled little pig, eyes squeezed shut, feet crossed in an oddly dainty way, made her want to cry. Everything today made her want to cry.

Sam had been missing since Friday night. She hadn't called all weekend, hadn't shown up anywhere. And the scream was playing over and over in Kirsten's brain. "There was a lot of background noise," she went on, "buses and cars. So I couldn't hear what she was saying. It sounded as if she was arguing, but I couldn't tell."

"Who was she arguing with?" Julie asked.

"I don't know!" Kirsten shot back. "I couldn't even tell if it was a guy or a girl. I probably could have figured it out, if I'd heard it again. I still can't believe I erased it!" She looked around at the girls at the table. "That's when I started calling you all—and I'm sorry, I know I didn't explain myself, but I didn't have time. I had to keep calling and find out if *anyone* had seen her."

"What did you find out?" Carla asked.

"Roger Cohen and Elissa Mackey saw her near Canal Street and the Hudson River—and

Gina Reese says she was dancing at a club in the meatpacking district," Kirsten said.

"I asked Dan Christensen, and he swore she was at a club on Avenue B," Julie admitted with a sigh.

Kirsten nodded. "And Trevor Royce thought she was at Sarabeth's Kitchen Saturday morning. The message was obviously left Friday night—so if she was at breakfast the next morning, she's probably okay, right? So then why hasn't she called? Why would she be in town and not call any of us or her mom?"

"Maybe she was eloping after breakfast," Leslie said, poking around the pig fetus with a forceps. "Um, what are we supposed to do with this piggie? Cut it up? I'm not in the mood for moo shu pork."

"Leslie, why are you in our group?" Julie asked.

"Let's get started, girls," Mr. Costas said, circulating around the room with a little smile on his face and a tweed jacket whose bottom hem was losing the battle with gravity. "And, er, don't *hog* the lab equipment."

Across the room, Jason Wolfe cackled.

"Good one, Mr. C!" It was safe to say that he'd probably win the distinction of being chosen Class Kiss-Ass at the end of senior year.

"Bobbi called me about a hundred times over the weekend," Kirsten went on, absently fingering the handle of the scalpel, "and I kept stalling. But I finally had to admit that I had no idea where Sam was."

"Oh my God, is that its *thing?*" Leslie said, taking a feathered clip out of her hair and putting it on a little flap of skin protruding from the fetal pig's abdomen. "It's cute."

"It's an *umbilicus*," Carla said, "not a *thing*. It says so right on the diagram."

"How can you possibly ever use that clip again?" Sarah asked.

Julie spread out the lab instructions. "Well, I'm worried. Really worried. I mean, the last time we saw Sam, she was leaving the Party Room with that strange older guy."

"He wasn't strange at all," Sarah said. "Hot, yes. Would I have gone with him? Yes. Might I have run off with him, forgetting to call my folks for a few days? Most definitely."

Leslie laughed. "You know, guys, this is *just* what she wants."

Julie glared at her. "What are you talking about?"

"Uh, is this Sam, or what?" Leslie replied. "Like, *shameless grab for attention?* Come on. When we were kids, like, when my little brother Jordan was a month old? One day Sam and I are playing in the living room—and the baby monitor's in there, too, connected to the little microphone thingy in his room, so you can hear him? So Sam sneaks up to Jordan's room, goes right up to the thingy, starts making baby noises and then choking noises and then horrible little screams, like, 'Get me out of here!' in this baby voice. Well, my mom comes into the living room at that moment and thinks it's Jordan and *totally freaks—*"

Mr. Costas sidled up behind them. As always, he wore a Harvard bow tie, which was kind of sad when you imagined that he must have once had great potential but ended up teaching biology at a prep school and doing lame stand-up comedy on Monday nights at clubs nobody had ever heard of. And to which none of the students ever went, of course. Very theatrically, he cleared his throat. *"Mademoiselles?"*

Carla batted her eyelashes. *"Pardon, le débauché de la mère."*

"Ah, oui," said Mr. Costas, looking a bit confused.

The girls huddled over the pig and tried to look terribly engrossed.

"What did that mean?" Julie asked.

"Motherf—," Carla began, but cut herself off as Mr. Costas turned back to them.

Kirsten forced herself to pay attention to the experiment. *Make first incision along dorsal side.* Following her lab notes, she picked up a scalpel and tried to figure out what *dorsal* meant.

"Hey, wasn't Sam doing it with some Yale guy?" Leslie whispered. "I'll bet he took her to, like, New Haven, Connecticut, or something."

"Julian's home for the semester," Kirsten said. "So yeah, anything's possible, but I doubt it. He was just a summer Nantucket thing. Sam got tired of Rolf saying she had a 'boyfriend in Jale,' and broke it off."

"Can we get off this topic?" Leslie said with a groan. "She's fine. If it isn't a prank—or even if it is—so what? Face it: We're all Woodley Bitches. It's not the first time Sammy Byrne

spent the weekend shacked up with some hottie, and it won't be the last."

Enough.

That had crossed the line.

"You're the only *bitch* at this table, Leslie. So shut up," Kirsten growled, stabbing the scalpel into the pig's side. *"Just shut up!"*

Julie, Carla, Sarah, and Leslie all stared at her, mouths agape.

Mr. Costas came running.

"Uh, Kirsten . . . ?" Julie squeaked.

"Is everything all right, girls?" said Mr. Costas, peering into the lab tray. "Who did that to poor Arnold?"

"It's the samurai dissection technique," Leslie said. "Kirsten got carried away."

Mr. Costas folded his arms. "Well, Kirsten, uh, we do prefer a more conventional lab technique at Woodley, but it looks like you won't be required to do it for the moment. I just received a note about you. The headmaster would like to see you in his office, right away."

Kirsten's mouth felt dry. She looked around at her friends. This was not good. Mr. Cowperthwaite never called you into his office unless there was a huge problem.

"Pig-stabbing infraction," Leslie said, but no one laughed.

"See you," Kirsten said, gathering her books. She stood and headed out the door and down the hall.

The Woodley School bio labs were in the new wing, actually the latest of four wings that had been added to the school's original somber Gothic building. It was built shortly after the Civil War by a financier named Alexander Chester Woodley III. The new buildings were attached to the old one in a kind of wheel with spokes, giving the school a feeling of, depending on who you talked to, a fortress (adults) or a prison (students). The playing fields were some of the only undeveloped land in the Bronx, and they lay just beyond a gentle hill with a small pond and a willow tree that had to be trimmed each year because its hanging branches hid more action than most of the clubs on West Street.

The principal's office was on the first floor, near the entrance to the old building, which you entered via a ramp that was like a tunnel back into time, into narrow hallways whose walls were lined floor-to-elbow-height with dark-stained oak and festooned above with commemorative plaques.

Mr. Cowperthwaite was standing outside the office, leaning against the wall, arm in its permanent crooked position as if still holding his beloved pipe that had been banned from school at least two decades ago. Next to him was a man in a navy blue suit, his eyes blue and half-lidded, sort of a Brad Pitt on a high-carb diet. And behind him were three New York City cops.

"Ah, Kristen," Mr. Cowperthwaite rasped, having never learned her name correctly after ten years. "This is Detective . . . uh . . ."

"Peterson," said Brad Pitt, flashing a badge. "Sorry to interrupt your day. We just wanted to ask a few questions about the disappearance of Samantha Byrne. Her parents filed a missing-person report this morning."

Kirsten swallowed. "Have you . . . found out anything?"

"Well, one lead so far," Peterson said, his blue eyes pinning her. "According to her parents, Ms. Byrne was last seen at your house."

6

Kirsten sank into a red
leather armchair that let out a slow, faintly
fartlike hiss. Being in the headmaster's
office without Mr. Cowperthwaite was
bizarre, to say the least. When Kirsten was
little, she thought he lived there. She still
suspected it.

But now it was just she and the cops.
Detective Peterson sat behind the tall oak
desk, putting his worn-out brown Florsheims
up on the ink blotter. He grinned, breathing in
the scent of leather, wood-polish, and ancient
pipe-tobacco. "Nice school. Hard to believe it's
the Bronx."

Behind him, two of the cops sat on the
padded seat in the window alcove, overlook-
ing the willow-draped slope of Woodley Hill.
"*Da* Bronx," one of them corrected Peterson.

Cop humor, Kirsten figured. The guy was

trying to lighten the mood, which she appreciated, sort of.

"It's actually Riverdale," Kirsten said. She hated this room. Just stepping in here made her feel as if she was in trouble. Of course, the fact that she was being investigated by the police didn't help.

"Let's cut to the chase, Kirsten," Peterson said, leaning forward. "I know you're nervous, so I'll make this short. Where exactly did Sam go after she left your house Saturday morning?"

Shit.

Shit, shit, shit.

All of Kirsten's lies were coming back to haunt her. Everything she'd told Bobbi.

Peterson was looking at her steadily. Professionally. Like he did this all the time and expected results. *If anyone can find Sam, I'm the man,* his gaze seemed to say. That part was a relief. A big relief. Even if Leslie was right, even if it was a prank, Kirsten's gut was telling her something *was* wrong.

The problem was Saturday morning.

What was she supposed to do—lie, and say that Sam had stayed at her house? Tell the truth, that she'd gotten stoned and drunk (*Yes, Officer, I am underage*) and then let her best friend walk into the night with a stranger? Either way, she was toast.

Okay, Kirsten, this guy is gathering information, she reminded herself. *The point isn't me. The point is Sam.*

She could fudge the rest.

"I—I personally don't know where she went Saturday," Kirsten said, "but I called some other Woodley kids, who said they saw her. . . ."

As Kirsten detailed each of the sightings, Peterson wrote them down on a legal pad. "And you began to suspect something was wrong when . . . ?"

"I heard this scream on my answering machine. It sounded like Sam, but I erased it by mistake—"

"Which was when . . . ?"

"Saturday morning."

Peterson leaned back, tapping his pencil on his chin. "So let me piece together the time line. Sam leaves your house Saturday morning after sleeping over. It must be fairly early, because that same morning, presumably after she's been out and about for a while, she calls and leaves a scream of terror—and even though you're home, the call goes to the answering machine. At some point you go to the machine, hear the message, and erase it—and you call other kids, who tell you they've sighted her at clubs. And these sightings all happen on Saturday morning, too, because after all, she's been at your house until then. Now, I'm kind of an old guy, so I don't know— are the clubs really open that early? Or, shall I say, that late?"

Kirsten gulped. She could see it now. Leg irons and stripes. Tearful visits with Mom across a Plexiglas barrier. That's where she was headed.

She swallowed again. This was insane. This was all her fault. If she *hadn't* covered for Sam, if she hadn't stalled for the *whole weekend*, Bobbi and Rolf would have called the police earlier and maybe Sam would be in school right now, in bio lab with Kirsten, all their friends, and the fetal pig.

Slowly, her head sank, her hair covering her face. "Okay, about Friday? Sam wasn't exactly at my house. She . . . didn't wake up there Saturday morning. . . ."

"I see. So . . . you were trying to keep her parents from freaking out? And that's why you lied?"

She peered up. Peterson's head was framed from behind by the huge Woodley grandfather clock, which now struck eleven, momentarily startling her but not affecting him one bit.

"Yes," she said, taking a deep breath. "Sam didn't come home with me . . . she wasn't at my house at all. I just . . . I assumed she was asleep at some friend's house . . . and all I had to do was make a few calls to find her. I didn't want to tell Bobbi the truth. I thought she'd get all upset and . . ." Kirsten's voice trailed off.

"And what?" Peterson said. "Call the police?"

All Kirsten wanted to do was cry. Like a fourth grader. "Yeah."

Peterson stood up. The other officers shifted to look at him as he came around the desk and knelt by Kirsten's chair. "Hey, you're not under arrest, Kirsten. I'm not interested in what you did at what party and at what time. And I don't care about the lies—covering to your friend's mom is not a crime. But it's not a good idea for your friend's sake, either. Trust me. You think you're doing her a favor, but you're not. You just get wrapped up in bigger and bigger lies. And before you know it, you're involved."

Kirsten was beginning to feel cold—cold and very alone. "*Involved? In what?*"

"Bad choice of words. Nothing yet," Peterson said. "Look, I'm just gathering information. My job is to get your friend back, that's all—so *we're on the same side,* okay?"

Kirsten nodded. *Involved.* The word was so ugly. "Okay . . . there was this guy at a bar, red hair, kind of cute, sort of rugged, wearing a Phish T-shirt, which seemed kind of strange because he wasn't the type. None of us had ever seen him before. He looked older, like college-age. Anyway, Sam was dancing with him, and then they left together—"

"She left the place, just like that, with someone she'd never met before?" Peterson asked.

Kirsten didn't like the implication. Sam loved to have fun, but she was *not* stupid, and despite what Leslie said, most definitely *not* a whore. "Sam and her boyfriend had just broken up, and she'd been upset, so maybe she wasn't totally her normal self. I think she was kind of glad to have someone new. And all they did was go outside. . . ."

Peterson scribbled something down. "Was he there—this boyfriend?" he asked, not looking up from his pad.

"Brandon? Yeah. Earlier. But he was gone by then. He was kind of loaded."

The detective looked up. "How did their relationship end? Was it mutual?"

Kirsten thought back to that night. "Not exactly," she said. "In fact, they had a huge fight on Friday. Brandon got a little carried away and freaked out on Sam."

Peterson was writing steadily. "So . . . have you ever talked to Brandon about this? Has he told you about his feelings? Would you say he has a grudge against her?"

"Sure. I mean, *she* was the one who broke up with him. He followed me home that night. Scared me half to death. He was mad crazy upset about the breakup—and about that guy she left with."

Peterson wrote some more, and then began pacing. He gazed out the window a moment, watching a couple—Winnie Forbes and Trey Gladstone, it looked like—walking slowly, lip-locked, across the field. "Tell me, Kirsten," he finally said, "was Sam unhappy at home?"

"Well, her dad left her mom for a Buddhist quilt-maker. They live in Vermont. Wouldn't that make you unhappy?" Kirsten shifted in her seat. Was he implying that Sam's home life would push her into self-destruction? That was absurd. "I mean, a lot of kids come from divorce, and they don't all disappear. What does her unhappiness have to do with it?"

"Just gathering background," Peterson said, scribbling a little more. "Is there anything else you want to tell me?"

Kirsten thought a moment, then shook her head. "Just one question, I guess. Do you get a lot of cases like this? And do you usually, like, *solve* them?"

Peterson stood, putting his notepad in a briefcase and signaling to the cops, who began heading for the door. "I'll be honest with you. Most missing-person cases tend to be run-aways. They leave home, upset about something, camp out with a friend, sleep in a park, whatever. Then, when they're tired of the rough life, it's back home to Mom and Dad.

Especially in cases like this, where there's just some minor family dysfunction. It's a classic scenario."

"Well, thanks, I guess," Kirsten said.

"Thank *you*, Kirsten, you've been a great help." At Peterson's signal, the uniformed officers went for the door. As they left, Peterson extended his hand to Kirsten. "Between you and me, I think your friend will show up in a couple of days."

Kirsten tried to smile. He seemed convinced. She wished she were too.

But the sound of the answering machine message kept replaying over and over in her head . . . the sound of that scream. . . . Why didn't the police think it was important enough to consider?

Peterson followed the other cops out. Kirsten heard them talking in muffled voices to Mr. Cowperthwaite in the hall. She waited. The last thing she wanted to do was see them again. The second to last thing was go back to the fetal-pig dissection.

She hung her legs over an arm of the chair and glanced out the window. It was a clear day, the pond rippling, the grass swaying gently. A flock of geese soared overhead, steadily south.

She caught sight of someone coming over the horizon—staying more or less hidden by the crest of the hill, probably cutting class. Kirsten liked to do that herself sometimes, just walk and walk in the fields without a care.

It was a girl, she could tell that, although she didn't know who. Silhouetted in the sun, the girl stopped and looked up, the morning light bouncing off her long platinum-blond hair.

She recognized the cut, just below the shoulders, and the confident flip of the head as the girl turned away and continued walking, downhill now, with a familiar stride, ever so slightly swaying at the hips.

Kirsten came slowly out of her chair and walked to the window for a better view. "Oh, my God," she whispered when she realized who the girl was.

Suddenly a smile burst onto Kirsten's face.

There was no mistaking any of it. This whole conversation with Peterson, the entire sleepless weekend, had been totally unnecessary.

Because her best friend was back!

Sam Byrne was back!

7

"Sam? *SPAMMIE!*" Kirsten cried.

The window was heavy. Like lifting her Gucci overnight bag on the way to a weekend in the Hamptons. Yes, Kirsten laughed at her own stupid thought. Stupid thoughts were great. Sam was back, making the world safe for stupid thoughts.

She squeezed under the sash, fell onto the grass below, and began running.

There she was. Wandering across the crest of the hill. CD player in her pocket, headphones on, swaying to the music. Picking dandelions and blowing on them.

So *Sam.*

So incredibly, wonderfully *Sam.*

Here at Woodley.

Where had she been? Why the hell hadn't she called? Was this her idea of a joke—making everyone crazy and then showing up one afternoon like Julie Andrews running across the Alps?

Kirsten ran up, stumbling over her own feet, not knowing whether to laugh, scream, or cry. She wanted to throw her arms around Sam, lift her in the air, and squeeze her to make sure she was real.

And *then* kill her.

Sam was looking in the other direction, lost in her music. Her outfit rippled in the wind, the dress they had picked out together at the Marc Jacobs show during Fashion Week.

Kirsten paused, catching her breath. Then, gently, she tapped her best friend on the shoulder. "Spammie, where the hell have you been?"

"Huh?" Sam turned around slowly, as if she'd expected Kirsten all along.

And Kirsten's smile fell. For a moment she couldn't say a word. It was as if someone had played a cruel joke with Sam's face, distorting it somehow. Her eyes were wrong, her mouth a little too big, the grin some kind of mockery.

"That is so funny you said that," the girl said.

Finally the voice connected with the facial features, knocking Kirsten into reality, making her realize that it wasn't Sam at all.

Not by a long shot.

"Emma?" Kirsten said, not wanting to believe it.

"Did you really, like, mistake me for Sam?" Emma giggled. "That is so weird. I guess it's the look, huh? Robert Swensen Salon. You *have* to go to him, Kirsten. He's expensive, but he's worth every penny." She twisted her newly dyed platinum hair around her fingers—the same way Sam always did.

Kirsten didn't know what to say. Emma's makeup was exactly the way Sam did hers: just a touch of pale pink lip gloss for daywear, her eyebrows plucked just so—enough to give them arc, but way short of the Martian look favored by the Long Island South Shore crowd. Again, Sam's exact technique. But the worst part was that Emma had gotten the *hair* right—the same blond shade, cut exactly to Sam's just-over-the-shoulder length.

And the sight of it made Kirsten short of breath, torn between the urges to cry, scream at Emma, or slap her.

But she did none of the above. She felt numb. This was just too weird.

"Emma, I'm sorry, but it's like you *copied* her," Kirsten said.

Emma shrugged. "It's just a look."

Okay, the girl had always been a little obsessed with Sam, but this was way over the top. "I think it's a little more than that," Kirsten told her. "How can I say this . . . do you really think that by doing this you'll magically be just like Sam? Because that's what it looks like. I mean, come on—you're *Emma Lewis*, okay? What's wrong with Emma Lewis?"

Emma turned in a huff, walking down the hill. "God, what grouch pill did *you* take this morning? I thought you, of all people, would *like* this look. Maybe you're just jealous. I'm sure Spammie won't mind when she sees me. She'll probably think it's cool."

"*You* don't call her Spammie," Kirsten snapped. Emma was totally over the line, and being polite was out the window. "Only her best friends do, and that will never in a million years be *you*. The least you can do is respect the fact that she's missing and not look as if you're trying to take her place!"

Emma stopped. She faced Kirsten with a blank, befuddled, very *Emma* look. "Sam is missing?"

"Open your eyes, Emma. Sam isn't in school today. She hasn't been seen since Friday night, when she left the Party Room. The police are here asking questions. Bobbi Byrne has filed a report. *I haven't slept in two days!*"

"Oh, no! Oh, my God." Emma dropped slowly to the grass as if her knees had given way. She started to cry. "No! Not Sam! No, please! Anybody but *her!*"

To say the least, it was not Oscar night.

Kirsten looked at her watch. She was not about to comfort Emma. She was going to go back to class, trust that Peterson was on the case and that Sam would be back soon.

"We're all broken up, okay, *really* broken up—all of us who *care* about Sam," Kirsten said, starting back to class. "So if you know of anything, call the police precinct and ask for Detective Peterson."

"I . . . I do," Emma said, her voice tear-choked and small. "I *saw* her, Kirsten."

Kirsten stopped in her tracks. She looked warily into Emma's eyes. Her patience for attention-grabbing was less than zilch. "You saw her? You saw her *where*, Emma? Did you see her after she left the Party Room?"

Emma smiled—an odd, far-off, private kind of smile. "I saw her in a dream. Saturday night. She had met some people. I couldn't tell who they were—nice people, traveling across the country, having adventures wherever they went. I don't know how they made a living or anything. Maybe they didn't have to. But Spammie was with them and having the greatest time. And just when I woke up, she turned to me and said, 'Tell them not to worry. Tell them I'm fine. I'll always be fine, and I'll always be thinking of them. . . .'" Emma raised her sleeve to her forehead dramatically, like something out of an old black-and-white movie. "And then it was over," she said with a sigh. "What do you think it all means, Kirsten?"

Kirsten was at a loss for words. She didn't believe in dreams coming true, especially Emma's insane dreams.

And at the moment, her eyes were on the shiny silver bracelet Emma was wearing on her wrist, which looked very familiar. In fact, it looked exactly like the antique bracelet Sam always wore—the one she'd inherited from her grandmother.

"Can I see that bracelet?" Kirsten asked.

Emma retracted her hand, hiding the jewelry. "Um, why? Why do you want to see it?"

"It's so beautiful," Kirsten said. "It also looks familiar."

"It's mine," Emma shot back. "It's *my* bracelet, and you can't have it."

Kirsten took a deep breath. "You stole it, didn't you?"

Emma's face reddened. And then she began to run.

Kirsten caught up with her halfway down the hill and spun her around. "How could you do that?"

"It's *my* bracelet, Kirsten," Emma insisted. "You want to take it, don't you? Well, I won't be talked out of it, and I won't sell it! You know how hard it was to find this?"

"It must have been really hard," Kirsten said. "What did you do, sneak into Sam's house at night? It's one of a kind, Emma. She told me that a million times. And she would *never* have given it to you."

Emma pulled back, looking at Kirsten as if she were crazy. "I bought it at East Side Jewelers. I can shop for jewelry too. I was looking for one exactly like Sam's. Is there anything wrong with that? Um, Kirsten? Are you, like, losing it?"

"You're dressed up as Sam, wearing Sam's jewelry, talking about your dreams of Sam—and accusing *me* of losing it?"

"The news about Sam is *very* stressful," Emma said. "You could see my dad, you know. He's a traumatic-loss specialist. When his patients get like this, he says—"

Kirsten didn't wait to hear the end of the sentence. As far as she was concerned, she'd be happy never to see Emma's face again. And if her dad was a famous shrink, it was no wonder the Upper East Side was so screwed up.

She ran down Woodley Hill and circled around the building to the main entrance. First period was just letting out. As she rounded the hallway to the science wing, Carla, Sarah, and Julie were rushing down the hall.

"Are you okay?" Julie asked.

"Fine, for someone who's just spent the last

half hour with a psychopath and a police detective."

"Did they find Sam?" Sarah added.

Kirsten shook her head. "He just asked some questions. Bobbi filed a report. Detective Peterson is on the case, but no, they haven't found her."

"They will," Carla said. "Or Sam will just show up on her own."

"Who's the psychopath?" Carla asked.

"Emma. I think she stole Sam's bracelet." Kirsten sniffed the air. Something smelled funky. "What's that stink?"

"Eau de Raw Pork," Sarah said with a look of disgust. "It's all over us."

Julie made a face. "And formaldehyde."

"Come with us," Carla said. "We'll have a ritual wash and some smokes to get rid of the stench."

Kirsten followed them into the girls' room, her brain straining with worry over Sam, anger with Emma, and a mixture of dread and hope over what Peterson would find.

She didn't smoke cigarettes. This morning, however, she would make an exception.

* * *

After school, Kirsten met Julie outside the old building in the Woodley courtyard. Cell phones weren't allowed in school, so no one had called Sam's house since lunch. Once you were outside, though, it was wireless heaven.

"Everyone's talking about Peterson," Julie said, moving away from the noise of the hundred or so conversations. "He kind of sucked the air out of the school. There are all these rumors about Sam."

Kirsten nodded. She'd heard them too. Sam was involved in a religious cult. She'd run away with a Norwegian prince. She'd wandered into Penn Station and fallen asleep on the Amtrak express to the West Coast. "Mr. Cowperthwaite looks like he aged ten years," Julie said. "He told me Peterson had called in some other kids to the office, but he wouldn't say who."

"Yeah, well, Leslie wasn't one of them. She wishes she were, though. She wants to marry Peterson and have tough little boys who will be movie stars and cast her as the sexy mom."

"Leslie is pissing me off almost as much as Emma." Kirsten took out her cell phone and began to tap out Sam's number. "Let me try her one more time," she said, even though deep down she knew that she wouldn't get an answer.

She'd just finished when Brandon rammed into her from behind.

"Ow. That *hurt*, you asshole!" Kirsten said.

"Nice vocabulary," Brandon muttered, looming over her like a sweaty bear. "I like a girl who talks dirty. Did you talk to Peterson that way?"

Kirsten gave Julie a look. Brandon's eyes were bloodshot, as usual, but he was also pale, and his navy blue Woodley uniform was wrinkled and kind of dirty—as if he'd been sitting in the fields smoking weed all day instead of being in class.

"Peterson called you in too?" Kirsten asked, backing away from him. She didn't like the way he was staring at her.

"Ohhhh, you're so surprised, aren't you?" Brandon said mockingly. "Think back. Remember what you told him about me. That I abused and threatened Sam. *Of course he called me in.* You made me sound like a freaky pervert!"

"I would never do that. It would give perverts a bad name." Kirsten put the phone to her ear, wanting him to just go away.

"I'm talking to you!" Brandon yelled, knocking the phone out of her hand.

Kirsten jumped away from him.

"Stop it!" Julie cried. "Brandon you're wasted."

"So what?" Brandon said with a guttural laugh. "I was wasted on Friday, too. But that doesn't make me a murderer. Does it, Kirsten?"

"Who said anything about—" She stopped.

Brandon lurched forward, backing Kirsten against a wall. Julie tried to push him away, but he was too strong. "You know what I think?" he said. "I think you two did it. You're her best friends. You let her leave there with that guy. You killed her."

"Sam is *not* dead!" Kirsten cried. "Don't even joke about that!" He was crazy. Kirsten looked around for help, but the phone callers were gabbing away on the other side of the building, and there were no faculty members in sight.

And now Brandon was pushing her— pushing her around toward the side of the building, behind the old hedges that badly needed trimming.

"Brandon, knock it off," Julie said, "or I'm going to get a teacher."

But Brandon's eyes were on Kirsten. "Yeah, good. Go ahead, Julie. You do that and leave us alone."

"Julie, don't!" Kirsten cried. She was shaking inside, but she tried to seem tough. She fixed her gaze on Brandon. "You lay a hand on me and you're dead."

"You don't scare me," Brandon said, his voice lowering to a whispery rasp. With every word, Kirsten could feel the puff of his hot breath on her cheek.

She tried to back away some more, but her heel caught on a crack in the pavement. She fell back, gasping, onto the asphalt of the faculty parking lot.

Brandon stood over her, his face a black shadow in the setting sun. "You'd better watch your back, Kirsten, because I'm going to do what you did to me. I'm going to trash your life. And when you least expect it, when everything seems to be going your way, you're going to pay. . . ."

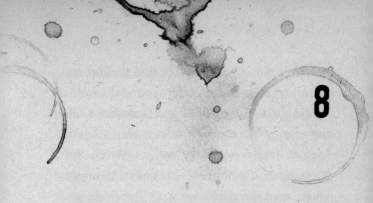

8

There was something slow and sleepy about the Party Room on a Monday night. It was a nice feeling, usually. But tonight, Kirsten thought, it felt sad and weird and empty, even with all her friends there.

Without Sam, the Party Room could never feel right.

Kirsten was still shaking from the afternoon. Brandon's threats echoed in her brain, scaring her, making her think about Friday night, about what he might or might not have been capable of doing. And then there was Emma, who was also a freak in her own right.

"Here, this will make you feel better," Julie said, bringing a small, cork-lined tray full of drinks to Kirsten, Sarah, and Carla at their table.

Julie had been the one to suggest coming

here tonight. At first Kirsten had said no, but the alternative was moping around the house in a state of panic. Mom and Dad were walking around like zombies, talking about Sam in hushed tones as if they really believed that Kirsten wouldn't be able to hear them. But she could, and she didn't want to. Anything was better than that.

"I can't believe you didn't nail Brandon," Carla said. "You should have kicked him where he lives."

Kirsten sipped her drink. It felt warm and soothing going down. "*You* try thinking of that when he's hovering over you."

"I never saw him like that before." Julie shook her heard. "It was as if something inside him just . . . snapped."

"Really?" Sarah said.

"Don't cross him . . . ," Kirsten said almost to herself. "I mean, he wigged out just because I mentioned him to Peterson. Imagine how angry he must have been at Sam when she broke up with him."

"Do you think he could have . . . ," Sarah said, her voice trailing off.

"*Brandon?*" Carla swallowed a sip of her

drink. "But I thought he loved her. That's why he was so upset when they broke up, right?"

Kirsten flinched, remembering Friday night all over again. Why hadn't she told Sam's parents the truth? Why hadn't she called the cops herself after Brandon had acted like such a basket case?

Because she was covering for her best friend, that's why. Sam would have done exactly the same thing for Kirsten.

"I don't want to think about it anymore," she said, and downed the rest of her drink.

"Yeah, hey, let's not get morbid about this," Julie said. "Detective Peterson told Kirsten that Sam probably just ran away. He's a pro. He knows. He has experience. And face it: Sam *is* unpredictable. So let's give him a chance. He's only been on it a few hours."

Carla finished her drink too. "You know, I'm thinking about Sam right now—about what she'd say if she saw us here like this. She'd laugh in our faces and tell us to get up and shake it!"

She got up from the table and began to groove, right there, all by herself, to the hip-hop song booming over the sound system.

Kirsten stood up, too, eyeing the door. Someone walked in, a guy she'd never seen before. "What if he shows up tonight?" she murmured.

"Brandon?" Sarah said. "If he does, we do to him what we did to Arnold."

"The fetal pig," Carla explained, slashing with her hand, *Psycho* style. "Eee, eee, eee, eee!" she screeched.

Sarah and Carla were not exactly the Sopranos, but it was nice to have someone covering your butt.

They all headed to the dance floor, but Kirsten's heart wasn't in it, and after a few minutes she left her friends and went to the bar. Hot Scott was there as always, polishing the already shiny wood. "Don't worry," he told her. "I'm sure they'll find her."

"Thanks." Kirsten nodded. "Hey, it's Monday after the weekend. Don't you ever get a day off?"

Scott smiled. "I need the cash. But I think I'll knock off Wednesday. Hump Day."

If Sam were here, she'd have something really smart to say about that, maybe involving the word *priapic*. "How about a pomegranate martini?"

"ID?" Scott asked with his trademark half-smile, and Kirsten flashed the lame card she'd bought as a joke in Times Square with Sam and Julie last July. Scott didn't even bother to look.

Yes, we love Scott, Kirsten thought as she watched him shake a mixture and pour it into a pretty glass. But no matter how much she tried, she couldn't get Sam and Brandon and all of it out of her mind—not even for a minute.

"Hey Kirsten, so who was the guy dancing with Sam that night?" Scott asked, writing out a tab. "The tall one with the red hair."

Kirsten shook her head. "Don't know much about him. Just that he left with Sam, and the police don't seem to think he had anything to do with her disappearance."

"I don't know, there's something about the guy that I didn't like," Scott said as he cleaned a few glasses. He paused. "Probably the Phish shirt."

Kirsten smiled. Leave it to Scott to lighten the mood a little. "Maybe you're right," she said. "Who likes that band, anyway? Granola heads."

"Well, I'll keep an eye out for him—and

nail him if he comes in here again." Scott gave her a long look, then quietly picked up the tab he had just written and ripped it in half. "This'll be on me, Kirsten. For all of you. On the house."

Kirsten's cheeks suddenly felt hot. "Thanks."

"Hey, I know how you feel. I had a friend like that once—would disappear, sometimes for weeks. High-school guy. Always came back, with a cowboy hat from Wyoming or a pound of weed from Mexico—never knew how he got to those places without a driver's license, but hey, he had a good time. We figured he wouldn't last through age twenty-five." Scott laughed, a sexy deep-chested guffaw. "Now he's the president and CEO of a Silicon Valley high-tech company."

"That makes me feel better. Maybe Sam will give me a job after college." Kirsten took a sip of her drink. It went down smooth. "Okay, I'm alive again."

Next to her, a soft male voice said, "I want what she's having."

Kirsten glanced to her left. A couple of barstools away, a guy sat down, all dressed in black. Silk shirt, cotton pants. He had dark brown hair, beautiful upward-arching eyebrows, and a nose that was so perfect, it had to have been sculpted.

"And one more for her," he added, smiling at Kirsten.

"You could be arrested for that," Kirsten said.

The guy smiled again. "Corrupting a minor? Well, I guess I'll just have to hold you here until the effects wear off. I'm Kyle."

"As in MacLachlan?" Kirsten cringed as the actor's name came out of her mouth, because first of all he was old and gray and not that good looking, in her opinion, and second of all the only reason she knew him was because she'd been forced to watch *Blue Velvet* by her film-freak ex-boyfriend Max Danson. Fortunately, Max had graduated but unfortunately, was last seen trying to get college girls to appear nude in a so-called student film. And third of all, while Kyle had redeemed himself on *Sex and the City*, *Blue Velvet* sucked, and this Kyle was much, much, *much* cuter.

"He's made some really good films. Didn't

love *Blue Velvet*, though," Kyle said. "And you are . . . ?"

"Kirsten."

"As in Dunst?" he asked.

Kirsten could live with that. "I guess so."

"She wishes she looked like you," he said, his smile spreading impossibly wide across his face, giving it a sort of sweet and tender openness.

"So does the other Kyle," Kirsten said.

"Wishes he looked like *you?*"

Kirsten blushed. "No—!"

"I didn't know this about him," Kyle went on, teasing her. "What magazines do *you* read?"

Kirsten laughed. *Laughed!*

Scott's back was to the CD jukebox, and in a moment a very slow romantic ballad was playing. Whistling softly, Scott began wiping the bar. He looked up at Kirsten and winked. "Great dance tune."

Kyle was already getting up from his stool. He reached out to her with just the right amount of confidence. He held her gently, body-to-body, as they danced across the floor.

Out of the corner of her eye, Kirsten could

see Carla, Julie, and Sarah huddled together and smiling at her. She closed her eyes and let thoughts of Sam and Brandon and Emma recede just for a moment. She hadn't felt this good in such a long time.

"Do you live around here?" Kyle said, in a voice soft and clear and delicious on the ear.

"Of course," she said. "I go to the Woodley School—well, maybe that doesn't mean anything to you. You're not from around here, are you?"

"What makes you say that?" Kyle asked.

"You're a guy, you're smart, and you're nice. They don't make them with that combination around here. I hear there are a few in, like, Wisconsin or something."

Kyle laughed. "Actually, I was born and raised here. Upper West Side. Sorry—I know to you Woodley girls, that knocks me down a peg."

"So do you go to college or something?" Kirsten asked. This guy was way too cool and mature to be in high school.

"Uh, Bowdoin College," he said. "You know . . . in Maine?"

"My mom thinks I should go to a college

down south, so she can be warm when she visits," Kirsten admitted. "What's it like at Bowdoin?"

"Well, at this time of the year, when the sun is still high in the sky, you can walk through Brunswick in your shorts and T-shirt, the heat on your face and the snow crunching under your feet—and it makes you feel so alive."

God, he was a poet, too. "You must be an English major."

"Political science," Kyle replied. "Actually I'm doing research on a seminar project. It's called 'A Marxist Analysis of Manhattan Elitist Society,' and I'm going to examine all the cultural tropes that signify class distinction and serve to stifle social mobility. Basically it's *Lifestyles of the Rich and Famous* for credit."

Smart. That was good. Kirsten liked smart.

As the song ended, Julie danced up close. "Hi, I'm Julie. Uh, Kirsten, I have to leave at ten? I think Carla and Sarah are going too. You can stay if you want. Are you okay?"

Kirsten nodded. "I'm fine." She could see Carla and Sarah standing near the door, looking on approvingly. Carla gave a subtle thumbs-up.

"She's cool," Kyle said, watching Julie walk away. "Is she your best friend?"

"Well, one of them . . . ," Kirsten said. Her friends were walking out now, and Kirsten imagined Sam with them. Sam would adore Kyle. If she were here, she would have made sure that Kirsten got every bit of contact information by now—phone, cell, e-mail address, IM buddy name. If you didn't have at least one guy's contact info by ten, it promised to be a loser of a night, in the World According to Sam.

In two hours it will be midnight. Almost Tuesday. Soon Sam will have been gone for three days, she thought.

"Kirsten . . . ?" Kyle said, touching her shoulder with concern.

"I'm . . . sorry," Kirsten said, looking up at Kyle, at his big, soft, basset-hound eyes, but all of a sudden she couldn't focus as tears spilled from her own.

"Are you okay?" Kyle asked. "Kirsten?"

She couldn't bring herself to put together the coherent explanation, because nothing made sense, the world had been turned upside down. So she followed her instinct and did the only thing that would make her feel better, which was to wrap her arms around his broad shoulders and kiss him, long and deep, so that someday, when everything was all right again and Sam had been found, she'd still have a good memory of this night.

"It's not you, Kyle," she said when they parted. "I just need to get out of here . . . alone."

Kyle reached into his back pocket, pulled out a pad of paper, tore off a page, and scribbled something on it. "Here's my cell. Call me, okay?"

Kirsten took the paper and put it in her pocket. Kyle was so wonderful and sweet and sexy, but she wasn't sure if she would ever call him. She was just too messed up right now. Too confused. She needed Sam back, safe and sound, and she couldn't think about anything else until that happened.

And then she was running across the floor, flinging her weight against the metal door latch, rushing out into the cool night to the sound of a deep snap that may have been the door opening or, just possibly, her soul breaking.

9

"I don't know his last

name," Kirsten said into the cell phone. As soon as she'd entered her building that night, she'd immediately called Julie, who was now pumping her with millions of questions as she rode up her elevator. "Just Kyle from Maine."

"Sounds like a toothpaste," Julie's voice replied. "I can't believe he's from so far away. He looks familiar."

"Actually, he's originally from New York City," Kirsten said.

"See? I never forget a face. I just don't know from what."

"Well, if he *has* been around New York, I don't know how I ever missed him." With a barely audible *ding,* the "PH" indicator lit up at the top of the polished-oak elevator panel. "More tomorrow," Kirsten whispered. "I'm home."

"Sweet dreams. *Really* sweet, if possible.

But don't do anything that requires the changing of sheets. Your cleaning lady already came."

"Shut up," Kirsten said. "Good night."

"Hey, Kirsten? Are you okay? Really? Because if you get lonely or sad, my mom's happy for you to sleep over—even in the middle of the night."

"Thanks, Julie."

She loved Jules.

Kirsten hung up just as the elevator door slid open. Mom had left a light on and a note:

DETECTIVE PETERSON CALLED TO LEAVE HIS DIRECT NUMBER. TURN THE LIGHTS OFF, PLEASE! ☺

The depressing mention of Peterson was almost made up for by the amusing idea that in a home that could fetch $9 million on the open market, Mom was worried about an extra three cents on the Con Ed bill.

Kirsten took the note, checked the answering machine—zilch—and sneaked through the house. Her room had been freshly made up by Marilena, the housekeeper, with new Ralph Lauren sheets turned back just so. A slight hum confirmed that Kirsten's iMac was still happily running on her antique desk.

Kirsten quickly undressed and, needing sleepwear appropriate to her desired mood, took out her slinky LaPerla negligee.

No, that wouldn't do.

Back in the drawer it went, and out came her soft flannel L.L. Bean jammies, the ones Marilena had bought her for Christmas last year. With a yawn, she went to her computer, which was covered with a cascade of IMs, mostly people asking about Sam. She'd left an Away message but she was in no mood to talk now, so she began closing them one by one.

Soon the last window was gone and she only had to deal with her e-mail messages. She hadn't checked them in a few days, so there were fifty-seven messages, mostly the usual stuff, cheap Vlagr@, pen1$ enlargement, breast enhancement, triple XXX chat rooms . . . *delete delete delete delete delete delete delete delete delete delete delete delete delete delete delete . . .*

Message fifty-six had a familiar "From" address—one that gave her a pang in the chest: bYrNiNgBuSh@rcn.com.

It was Sam's address. Probably one of the fifteen or so lists of jokes and weird Web site links Sam had sent last week.

Kirsten squinted at the date on the message, her finger poised to delete again, but she froze.

It was today's date. The message had been sent early this morning.

"That's impossible," Kirsten murmured. "Sam's been gone since Friday. . . ." Then she gasped. "Unless Sam is really okay!"

Her hand shook as she brought the cursor to the message and wondered *why?* Why the hell hadn't she called? *Why e-mail?*

It didn't matter. She clicked on Sam's address. Instantly the message blinked onto the screen.

From: spammie byrne (bYrNiNgBuSharcn.com)
To: kirsten sawyer
(lesbiches326ahotmail.com)
Subject: hey there babes!
hey kissyface, wazzup!!!! evrything fine wid
me so dont worry.....like that guy
singz.....dont worry b happy.....u no the
one with the dreds whashisname i foget?? ;0

whatever! lol not home now, will be
soooon....dont tell Bobbi yet ok. cu &
ttfn!!!!
xxxxxxxxxoooo spam

"I don't BELIEVE it!" Kirsten shouted.

She leaned down and kissed the iMac right
on the seventeen-inch adjustable flat-panel
display and she didn't care if she left a greasy
lip mark that would drive her crazy tomorrow.

Sam was okay!

She had to talk to her right now. Grabbing
her cell phone, she tapped Sam's number.

"Kirstie?" Mrs. Sawyer called. "Is that
you?"

"Yeah, I'm home!" Kirsten called out.

"Are we forgetting, tomorrow is a school
day!"

No kidding, Kirsten did not say. "Okay . . .
sorreeeee. G'night."

Two. Three. Four. Mom was asleep.

Sam's line was ringing now.

*"Hello, um, yeah. Sam here. Go ahead and
talk—"*

Voice mail. Damn.

Kirsten waited and said, "I got your e-mail.

We need to talk—mucho madness. Call me!"

Then she sat back at the computer and typed:

```
From: kirsten sawyer
(lesbiches326@hotmail.com)
To: spammie byrne (bYrNiNgBuSha@rcn.com)
Subject: Re: hey there babes!
WHERE R U???????????????? :(
```

As the message went off into cyberspace, Kirsten waited and watched. She checked her buddy list, but Sam was off.

For the first time ever, she wished she were a geek. Carla would have been able to look at the headers, or whatever they were, and find out exactly where this message came from, what time Sam wrote it, and what she was eating.

Kirsten scanned Sam's message again. Having her words, right in front of her, was so comforting.

Her words . . .

Something about them was funny. Kirsten read through the message again, and her excitement began to lose its edge. It was the right address, so it *had* to be from Sam—but something was off. Something in Sam's words.

The third time through, Kirsten's heart began to sink. She had exchanged a million messages with Sam, give or take a few. And she knew all Sam's tricks. All the ways she expressed her Sam-ness online. Yes, this message was from Sam's e-mail address, all right.

But . . . it wasn't from Sam.

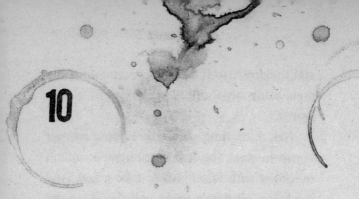

10

"Settle down, kids," Mr. Costas said at the beginning of the next day's bio lab. "Get into your lab groups and be serious. No *hamming* it up!"

Kirsten was in no mood for bad jokes about fetal pigs. She dragged herself to the lab table, where the shriveled little specimen awaited them. Sarah, Carla, Leslie, and Julie gathered around her.

She was feeling raw. She'd hardly slept again, getting up several times in the night to reread the message, hoping she'd change her mind, hoping to find a sure sign that Sam *had* written the note. But she just became more and more convinced that it was a forgery.

Why? The question haunted her. What kind of person would forge an e-mail message from Sam?

Julie spread out the experiment's instruction sheet on the table. "Keep telling us about the e-mail, Kirsten," she said, eyeing Mr. Costas as he walked away. "I can listen and do this stuff for the report. . . . 'Examine aqueous contents of eye.' This ought to be fun."

Kirsten lowered her voice to a whisper, continuing a conversation they'd begun before class in the hall. "Well, I realized the message *couldn't* have been from Sam, and I forwarded it to Detective Peterson. He called me right back on the cell. I couldn't believe he was awake. He asked me all kinds of questions that I didn't know the answer to, technical stuff. He said he wants to see the headers or something, so I told him I'd ask Carla."

"Just a minute." Taking a scalpel, Julie carefully lanced the pig's eye.

"Ohhh . . . ," Sarah groaned, holding her stomach. "Someone call PETA."

"How can you do that?" Leslie asked, turning green.

Kirsten looked away. "What confuses me is that it comes from Sam's e-mail address—but Peterson says it's possible to steal an e-mail address. Is that right, Carla?"

Carla nodded. "Just a matter of setting up

an account with your own POP and SMTP protocols but spoofing the reply-to. Anyone can do it."

"In my sleep," Sarah muttered.

"But . . . 'kissyface'?" Julie said. "No one but Sam calls you that."

"True, but people have ears—someone else could *know* about it," Kirsten replied. "It was the other stuff, in the subject line and at the end of the note. Sam *never* calls me Babes. And all that crap—ttfn, the emoticons—she wouldn't be caught dead writing that. We always make fun of kids who think it's cool to use those things."

Sarah frowned. "Wait. It isn't?"

Mr. Costas sidled by, looking over Carla's shoulder. "Very good. And remember, the sagittal section of the fetal pig is *not* the Central Pork. . . ."

Carla rolled her eyes.

Mr. Costas smiled proudly, and Julie read the next part of the instructions. "'Open thoracic cavity and remove organs for examination, as per instructions . . .'"

As Julie went to work, Kirsten looked away. "I dreamed about Sam all night," she said. "I just couldn't figure out *who* would do something like steal Sam's e-mail address—and *why?* It's perverse. And so I'm thinking about this over breakfast and reading the Metro section of the *Times*, page three, and I see this article—something like 'Upper East Side socialite daughter reported missing after late-night carousing at notorious teen gathering place. . . .'"

"That sucks," Sarah said.

"Maybe not," Carla replied. "The more people who know about Sam, the more who know what she looks like, the better chance of finding her."

"Did they really say 'gathering place'?" Leslie asked. "Makes it sound like the Mouseketeers headquarters—only without Justin."

"Peterson says the press coverage can be bad news," Kirsten added. "The runaways know they're being chased, so they go further undercover."

"Well, *I* saw it on the local morning news," Sarah said. "They mentioned the mystery man. Gave a description, too. Red hair and all, even in the Phish T-shirt."

"Do you think she married him in Vegas, like Britney?" Leslie asked brightly.

"You are sick," Julie told her as she made incisions through the aorta and pulmonary artery, reached in, and carefully lifted out the pig's heart. "Could you hold this for me?" she asked, turning to Leslie.

"Mglfff!" Leslie clapped a hand over her mouth and ran from the room.

Kirsten stared at the little rocklike organ in Julie's gloved hand. It didn't look revolting at all, just small and tough.

"Guess the little piggy doesn't have to worry if its heart will ever be broken," Emma's voice said softly from behind.

Kirsten, Carla, Julie, and Sarah turned. Emma was standing there, with a little smile, in all her wannabe-Sam glory.

"You decided not to cut class today?" Kirsten asked.

Emma nodded. "Don't mean to interrupt, guys," she said, drawing her perfect platinum hair behind her ears. "I just wanted to say I'm sorry, to Kirsten. I didn't mean to yell at you."

Kirsten noticed that Emma's wrist was bare. "What? No bracelet today?"

"I didn't want to get into an argument. I've had enough of that. Look, we're all in this together now—you, me, all of you guys. I mean, we were always in different circles, but sometimes you have to look past that. I'm sad too. We've got to be like sisters at a time like this."

Julie set the heart down, and the girls looked at one another uncomfortably. Emma sat on Leslie's vacated stool, but no one had the urge to tell her to go.

"I'm having trouble with the lab," Emma went on. "I don't know, I guess I'm not cut out for dissection."

"That was a bad joke," Carla said dryly. "'Cut out'?"

"Ugh. I didn't mean it like that," Emma said. "It's just gross. And the smell."

Kirsten sighed. "I think it's disgusting too."

"Well, today's your lucky day," Emma said. "I told Mr. Costas that I had a religious objection to the dissection. The teachers are trained to take that kind of thing seriously. Even Mr. Comedy Central. So he said that if anyone wanted, we could get together and do a report with diagrams instead."

"Fine with me," Sarah said.

Emma was smiling, and in the white-green reflection of the overhead fluorescent lights, her makeup was a little too pale, her hair color a little too fake. But Kirsten had gotten used to that by now.

She was kind of weird, yeah, and Sam had always disliked the girl, but frankly, all of their lives Kirsten had felt a little sympathy for Emma. She was clearly messed up, without a sense of self, blah blah blah, but until now totally harmless. So, what if she was telling the truth? What if she had bought a close knockoff of Sam's bracelet? What if this psycho obsession was just a phase, on her way to some other obsession, with Elvis or Avril Lavigne or something? And wasn't there an old cliché . . . something about the better the shrink, the weirder the kid? Emma had that on her plate too.

"Thanks," Kirsten said. "That's nice of you, Emma."

"Hey, anytime, sister-girl." Emma put her arm around Kirsten's shoulders.

Sister-girl? Kirsten turned. Another phrase that was signature Sam.

No one made a move to go off and write that separate report. Instead, they all watched as Julie held out the instruction sheet and read aloud the next step in the lab: "'Removal and inspection of joints . . .'"

Emma made a face. "Well, Doctor, I'm out of here. Kirsten, come join me. I'm going to the library to start research."

"I'm with you," Sarah said, looking ambivalent but glad to get away from Arnold.

"You're abandoning me?" Julie asked.

"I'm going to be an English major," Sarah said. "This is irrelevant to my education."

"I'll stick around," Carla said.

Kirsten laughed. "Me too. As long as I can stand it."

"Okay, well, see you later!" Emma said cheerily.

As the two girls left, Kirsten felt uncomfortable. Sam had said something Friday night that had stuck in her head. Something about Emma. *"One day she's going to make all of you into her best friends, then bump me off so she can take over my life."*

It had been a joke. No one had taken it seriously, of course. But as Emma headed for the door, Kirsten noticed something new. A pair of earrings that looked like intricate little antique grapes dangled from Emma's ears.

Kirsten had seen them before too. Sam had a pair. They matched her grandmother's bracelet.

"I just wanted to say I'm sorry," Kirsten said to Kyle from across a table at Jackson Hole on Second Avenue. She nervously unfolded her napkin and placed it on her lap. "For running out on you at the Party Room, I mean."

Julie had finally convinced her to call him after school that day—saying that Kirsten would always be wondering "what if?" if she didn't. Which was true. So she did, and there they were. Kyle had suggested meeting at this place, and now Kirsten was feeling weird and embarrassed for having run out of the Party Room like some crazy and dramatic lunatic.

But he didn't know about Sam, so he couldn't have understood her mood that night. He deserved an explanation. Although the clatter and bustle of a burger joint was not exactly an intimate setting, and the background music was the third inning of a base-

ball game from the wide-screen TV above the
bar, it was okay. Jackson Hole was always full
of Woodley kids. And they served cheap pitch-
ers of beer.

Sarah was sitting with Trevor Royce in the
back, and a table full of kids from the debate
team were noisily discussing foreign policy or
something near the door. Jackson Hole was
right up there with the Party Room in the
home-away-from-home category.

Kyle was wearing a baseball cap and dark
glasses. He smiled curiously. "I was alone on
an elevator in an office building once. Big,
roomy elevator, and I was in the back. The
door opens, and there's this woman—like,
maybe in her early twenties. She runs in,
really quickly, and goes, 'Sorry!' And I'm like,
'That's okay.'"

"And . . . ?" Kirsten said.

"And . . . I'm thinking, what was she sorry
about? We were doing exactly the same thing,
using the elevator to get down to the street.
So . . . I was wondering, do you think that it's
a chick thing—you know, to apologize all the
time? Like, you've been trained to automati-
cally think of the other person's comfort?"

"A *chick* thing?" Kirsten repeated.

Kyle blushed. "Sorry, I didn't mean to be offensive. My theory is that guys go too much in the other direction—always looking after themselves first. Oh God, I'm alienating you. I get nervous when I'm around beautiful, smart girls and I don't have any idea what to talk about. Okay, what I *meant* to say was, no need to apologize. I wasn't offended. Not even a little."

Kirsten had to laugh. Kyle was cute when he was nervous. She instinctively reached across the table and touched his hand reassuringly. How could he think she minded a guy actually taking the time to think about how a *girl* thought? "Monday night, I was . . . not in the greatest mood," she said. "Some really bad personal things have happened."

Kyle's face darkened. "I'm sorry . . ."

"Maybe you've seen the news reports about the missing girl," Kirsten said.

Kyle winced. "You knew her?"

"She's my best friend," Kirsten said.

The waitress swooped down, placing plates in front of them. "Kaluba burger . . . Woulia Boulia salad . . ."

As they began eating, Kirsten spilled the whole story to him—the details of Friday night, the scream on the answering machine, the weekend of back-to-back phone calls, Peterson's interrogation, Emma's weird behavior, and Brandon's threats.

Kyle listened. He was a great listener, looking at her with rapt attention, asking gentle questions, his eyes still and sympathetic. Kirsten hardly knew him, but she felt she could talk to him about anything. "No wonder you were feeling so bad, Kirsten," he said. "That's a lot to deal with . . . so much uncertainty."

Kirsten sighed. "I'm worried about *everything.* That strange guy she left with . . . I mean, no one's ever seen him, before or since. But then there's Emma, and I don't know if she's a harmless dweeb or a psycho thief. Who knows? She could have Sam tied up in a spider hole, feeding her mice while writing a ransom note—*I don't know!*" Kirsten took a deep breath. She was going overboard. It was the lack of sleep. And the uncertainty, Kyle was right about that. "I'm sorry, Kyle, I didn't mean to go off like that."

"Hey. Apologies not necessary, remember?" Kyle looked up. "Someone's waving to you. Over by the door."

Kirsten turned to see Emma waving and grinning a Sam-like grin and wearing a jacket similar to the one Sam had bought at Barney's last month. She was arm in arm with some guy, blocked from Kirsten's view, at this angle, who was now whispering into Emma's ear. Summoning up all her good manners, Kirsten waved back, and it occurred to her that since Sam's disappearance, Emma was the only girl who had seemed consistently in a good mood.

The waitress pointed Emma to a table at the opposite end of the restaurant, and as the happy couple turned toward it, Kirsten saw who Emma's partner was—*Brandon.*

She felt ill—as if she was going to lose it right into her Woulia Boulia salad. "That's Emma . . . *and* Brandon," she told Kyle. "This is so sick. Brandon didn't know Emma existed! She must have jumped on him. She's stolen Sam's look, and now she's trying to steal her boyfriend—I mean, her ex-boyfriend."

"Bizarre," Kyle said, jockeying in his seat for a clearer look at the couple.

The baseball game suddenly gave way to the sharp trumpet blare of a special news report. *"Good evening,"* an anchorman said. *"Tonight we have the latest on the Missing Preppy Case. . . ."*

There, above the bar, in full life-size color, was Sam. With that megawatt smile, frozen in time on the day they'd taken the school pictures in Central Park. The image faded, and a new one took its place, a drawing this time.

"Samantha Byrne was seen leaving an uptown club with a man who looks like this," the reporter announced. *"Persons with any knowledge are urged to contact the New York City Police at once."*

It was a police sketch. A man with fat cheeks, a scraggly beard, heavy eyebrows, and red hair.

Totally not right. *So* not right.

Kirsten shook her head. "No. He didn't look like that at all. He was younger. Thinner and better looking. I gave Peterson a description of that guy—it wasn't at all like that. . . ."

More Woodley kids were in the restaurant now, and Kirsten could see their faces, all around—staring at the screen, eyes red, looking at Sam, looking at her—all the pity, the whispers, the attempts to figure the identity of a man who was not the right guy . . . and in the background, the sound of Emma's voice, chattering away, talking about Sam, Sam, Sam.

It was too much. Too much talk and hand wringing and misunderstanding. She had to do something. Sitting back and waiting for the cops to bring Sam home wasn't enough. She stood up from the table, averting her eyes from Kyle's bewildered glance. "Sorry, Kyle," she said, "but I have to get out of here."

"But where are you going?" he asked.

"The police are looking for the wrong guy. I'm going to call Peterson and give him the description again. And then I'm going to look myself. I know the places Sam likes. I'm going to go to every one of them and search in every dark corner until I find him."

Kyle stood. "Kirsten, I know you're upset, but I don't think that's a good plan. It could be dangerous."

He looked so concerned. She was leaving him again, just the way she'd done at the Party Room. "I can't *not* do it," she said softly. "I owe it to Sam. I can't just stand by anymore."

"I'll go with you," Kyle said.

She thought about it briefly, but shook her head. At this point, her trust in fellow human beings was at an all-time low. "No," she said firmly. "I need to do this alone."

Kyle took a deep breath and nodded. "Okay. I understand. But promise me you won't do anything crazy when you're out on your own."

Kirsten nodded and attempted a smile. "I won't. Promise."

As she took her coat and left, she intended to keep her promise. She wouldn't do anything crazy on her own. She would get Julie to go with her.

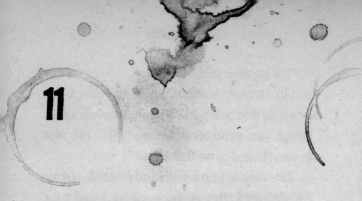

11

I'm so proud of myself.

Really proud.

I am keeping my impulses in check.

Control is important.

I will take my time with this one.

Change happens with time. Time and patience.

And control.

Let's face it. It's nice to have someone to talk to at a party.

An intimate conversation among friends. I could get used to this.

"Now, some of the girls I know," I tell her, "they have big mouths. Or they can be sweet, with good hearts, but they are not nice to animals? I don't get it? Do you get it? I bet you think I'm an animal, don't you? DON'T YOU?!

Silly, she can't answer you. She's got a handkerchief in her mouth!

But you do crazy things when you're in a good mood.

And when you're sucking on nitrous oxide to disguise your voice.

To make it sound all squeaky. It's funny.

I think about turning off the TV. The nightly news reports have ended, but you never know when they'll break in again. Got to keep up with the news.

"Now, I have a theory," I tell her. "Want to hear it? Here's what I've learned. Some people think they can get away with treating the animals like crap. But they're cowards! This time they'll learn their lesson. You watch. They'll hover around a little, but ultimately they're too afraid to come inside and join the party . . . because they know if they get too close—smash! Like mashed potatoes."

Mashed potatoes.

There are mashed potatoes in the fridge.

Hmmm.

It is past dinnertime—way past dinnertime. My, how time flies when you're having fun, but the old tummy is rumbling and WHAT KIND OF HOST DOESN'T OFFER A GUEST DINNER AT DINNERTIME?

"Be right back. And . . . don't go away!"

Don't go away. Ha. Right.

A laugh a minute. We are having fun now, aren't we?

There they are. Back of the fridge, in the container.

Into the microwave. Add salt. Mashed Potatoes setting . . .

Another hit of nitrous oxide . . . no use sounding like me. Yet.

"Ah, voilà! Doesn't that smell good?"

Idiot. She still has a handkerchief in her mouth. You put it there so she wouldn't make noise. Well, she can't eat with a handkerchief in the mouth either, Einstein . . .

"Out it comes! Now keep quiet if you want mashed potatoes, made by my mom with a special family recipe!"

"WHAT THE HELL DO YOU THINK YOU'RE DO—"

"Handkerchief back in! Bad girl, Spammie, now breathe . . . two . . . three . . . four. . . . Shall we try again?"

I pull out the handkerchief. Not so glam now. It's a sad sight, really. Her mouth is dry and cracked. A little red at the corners. Maybe it's an allergic reaction to the laundry detergent. Shouldn't use that cheap Arm & Hammer shit anymore.

Ah well, this treatment is temporary. She won't need a handkerchief when I'm through, will she? No, she won't need it at all.

At least she's quiet now.

One spoonful.

"Mmmm. Mmmmm, is it good?" I ask.

"Yes, yes, it's good," she says.

She likes it. SAM LIKES IT!

I bow, which is ridiculous, because she still has the blindfold over her eyes so she can't see me. And clumsy me, I drop a lump of the precious potatoes right in her lap. "Oops. Sorry."

"Those are brand-new pants," Sam says. "I can get the stain out in the bathroom with a little shampoo. It's amazing how that works—"

"Really? OH, REALLY?" I shouldn't get so angry. But she's trying to scam me. She must think I'm a moron. "And what ELSE will you do if I untie your hands?"

"Look, what I'm trying to say is . . . I have to go to the bathroom," she says. "It's an emergency, okay?"

"That's what this pot is for," I say calmly,

because I have heard this crap before.

"Well, yeah, that—but there's something else, okay? It's not something you can do for me, and it's private, and you know exactly what I mean— now, you don't have to give me my bag, but if you give me what I need from the bag, I'll take it in and come back and spare your floor from leaking into your neighbors downstairs, who I'm sure would not take kindly to it. Hey, look, I'm not going any- where, all right? Do you hear me screaming and carrying on?"

Sigh. Oh, all right. I understand. I get closer, pulling my trusty Swiss Army knife from my pocket. "You know what happens if you try any- thing. . . ."

I reach around and undo the knot, but it's a good knot . . . it's a TOO GOOD knot, and I'm wondering if I just use that knife and get some more rope, but rope has gotten expensive, at least this kind. . . .

"Owwwwww!"

I'm on the floor.

She kicked me.

THE BITCH KICKED ME!

And now she's raising her arms. She's doing it. She's removing the blindfold.

"Oh my God . . . ," she says. "It's you. I don't believe it's you."

Stupid.

How unbelievably stupid.

I push her back onto the chair. She tries to fight back, but she's not as strong as I am and if she had THOUGHT OF THAT IN THE FIRST PLACE, I wouldn't have to do this.

"LET ME GO!" she shrieks.

I'm feeling sad.

She didn't know how to follow directions.

All we needed was some time.

She didn't get that little fact.

JUST A LITTLE TIME, THAT'S ALL.

"I'm sorry," I say. "We would have been a good team if you weren't so OUT OF CONTROL. I can't let you go now. It was too early. You saw my face, and it was too early to do that. ALL I WANTED WAS FOR US TO BE FRIENDS AND TO LEARN A LITTLE SOMETHING ABOUT LOYALTY, BUT YOU SAW MY FACE!"

What can I do? I have no choice now. . . .

12

"That's the place," Kirsten said, looking at the faded remnants of painted letters—CUTS—on the wall of a grimy warehouse down the block, under the abandoned elevated freight train in New York's old meat-packing district.

She and Julie had been to four clubs already, dropping a wad on drinks that they either had to chug or leave behind. No luck so far. This was the last place Kirsten could think of, a place Sam went to only in her craziest moods.

They passed couples making out in the old truck docks, and were winked at by a person of indeterminate gender wearing lurid makeup and few clothes. Against the night-black support beam for the elevated train, a rail-thin guy was snorting something from the palm of his hand, and Kirsten thought she saw reflected in the streetlight a hypodermic needle passed among a crowd near a parked Lexus. Beneath their feet the sidewalk was slippery. Once last summer Sam had gleefully explained that the pavement was permanently saturated with the fat left by slabs of beef dragged by truckers across the sidewalks.

Back in those days, though, the pavement probably didn't bounce with a pounding hip-hop beat like it did tonight.

"Sam used to go *here?*" Julie asked.

Kirsten nodded. "As a last resort." It wasn't her favorite place either. She and Julie breezed past a line of less-than-fashionable waiting forlornly behind the velvet rope. They waved at the bouncer, a beefy guy chewing gum, who barely looked up from his paperback copy of *The Fountainhead.* Kirsten had dressed in her tiniest Prada tank, which pretty much guaranteed admittance anywhere, even here, even if the gate people didn't know her.

"We're looking for a college guy with scruffy red hair!" Kirsten yelled over the noise coming from within. "Might have been wearing a Phish T-shirt!"

The guy shrugged, gesturing to the door.

"Go on in, if you want. Have a look. . . ."

"Thanks." Kirsten gave him a small business card, her dad's, with his info crossed out and her own name, cell number, and e-mail address written on back. "Please call if you see anyone like that."

Kirsten and Julie descended a black metal staircase that clanked and shook as they walked, down into a dance floor that crawled with bodies. The bass was like a physical assault, like something injected straight into the bloodstream. On any other night it would have been impossible to resist the urge to dance, but tonight Kirsten and Julie elbowed their way through the sweaty, pumped-up crowd. On the walls, which seemed to stretch the length of a football field, vast screens played scenes from *Reservoir Dogs, Bonnie and Clyde, The Silence of the Lambs*—gun violence, amputation, and cannibalism as background. From the ceiling hung thick metal hooks, chutes, and curved tracks left over from meat-processing days, not used as decoration, and it made Kirsten think of helpless pigs and cows floating through the air on their way to shrink-wrapped meal-sized portions.

"I DON'T SEE HIM!" Julie shouted over the noise.

"COME WITH ME TO THE BAR!" Kirsten replied.

"I'M NOT STAYING HERE. DON'T ORDER DRINKS!" Julie said.

The bartender had massive shoulders that could have been sides of beef themselves. Kirsten caught his attention, leaned over the bar, and once again gave a description of Erik the Red.

"Oh. This is the guy on the TV?" he said.

"Exactly. But he really doesn't look like that—"

"Thinner, right? Younger. Like, twenty-two, twenty-three?"

"Do you know him?"

"Maybe. There is a guy comes here who has this really red hair. Spends a lot on drinks. I think he hangs at Mole, too. Over on West Street near Little West Twelfth. I saw him there when I was subbing one night. Anyway, I'll keep my eye out here, too."

"Thanks!" Kirsten handed him a card.

Mole. She didn't know that place at all, but for the first time, they had a lead. She felt a flicker of hope. "This is great," she said.

Julie slumped onto a stool. "What's so great? There are thousands of guys with red hair. We can't go to *every* club. This is like finding a needle in a haystack. Let's go home."

Kirsten glanced around, surveying the faces that swung in and out of the flashing lights. They hadn't found the guy, true. But she didn't believe the trip was a total failure. They'd planted seeds. Created a buzz. The bartenders and bouncers in all of Sam's favorite places had Kirsten's card and knew how to reach her.

"Hey," said a deep voice behind Kirsten.

She turned to face a guy about six feet five, with sunglasses and spiky black hair and enough hardware pierced into his face to stock a small jewelry store. He grinned wordlessly at Kirsten, until she realized he was holding his hand out to her.

In his palm were three small blue pills. "Free, for you. If you dance with me."

Julie rolled her eyes and grabbed Kirsten's hand. *Out of here*, she mouthed.

They both bolted from the bar.

"Bitch," the guy called out.

They made their way back upstairs and onto the street. "Can we go now?" Julie said, storming into the street to hail a cab.

"Just one more place," Kirsten said. "Mole. It's not far."

A taxi veered over to Julie, and she pulled open the back door, looking tired and exasperated. "Kirsten, I want to find Sam. I want to try to get this guy and ask him questions. But New York is too big to do this kind of stuff. We could be out here all night and still not scratch the surface of all the clubs and bars. I'm heading home. Come home with me, okay? We're not helping Sam by running ourselves ragged."

Kirsten wanted to go home, too, but she couldn't. If she didn't look, if she didn't try one last place, she'd never forgive herself. What if he was there? What if she missed him and could have found out the crucial bit of information about Sam?

It wouldn't take long, she promised herself. A quick look, and she'd catch a cab back home.

"It's okay, you go ahead," she said to Julie. "I won't be long."

Julie hesitated, then got into the cab and

closed the door. "I don't feel good about this," she said. "I already have one missing friend."

Kirsten smiled. "I'm not going anywhere, not with anybody. I just want to look at the place. I promise, I'll call you as soon as I leave the club."

"You promise?" Julie asked, and Kirsten nodded.

As the cab sped off, Kirsten headed down West Street. It was dark but full of people. Just ahead, the sidewalk was clogged with motorcycles in front of a biker bar. Men with beards and potbellies eyed her as she passed, and a punked-out stoner with a shaved head and a studded color called out, "Peace, you guys!" and started laughing.

At the corner of Little West Twelfth, a couple leaned against a big black Escalade, French-kissing and moaning. The car was nice, and reminded her of the one Brandon drove around whenever his dad let him. . . .

She stopped in her tracks. It *was* Brandon leaning against the car. The same blunt profile and leather jacket, the same wavy black hair.

He came up for air, and Kirsten heard his guttural, low-throated laugh. It was joined by a dreamy cooing noise that sounded a lot like Sam, but Kirsten knew to expect that by now from Emma.

Kirsten veered into the street to avoid them, but it was too late. "Kirstennnn! Hiyeee!" Emma called out.

"Hey, Emma," Kirsten said.

"Look what the wind blew in," Brandon said. "Looking to score some weed, Kirsten? Or are you checking up on me for Peterson? Why don't you stick around awhile, maybe I'll commit a murder for you."

Emma put a finger to his lips. "Come on, Brandy Alexander, be nice."

Brandy Alexander? Kirsten cringed. That was what Sam used to call him. "You don't miss a thing, Emma. Not even a nickname," she said.

Brandon pushed Emma aside and began striding toward Kirsten. "I think you are following me, aren't you? You want to pin Sam's disappearance on *me.* You are one sick bitch, Kirsten. You know that? I don't like people like you. I don't like you at all."

He was moving fast toward her now, nearly jogging. The veins in his neck were taut, his eyes bloodshot. He was reaching into his pocket.

Kirsten backed away, turning her ankle on the curb. She cried out in pain, stumbling into the street.

"Brandon, what are you doing?" Emma cried out. *"Come back here!"*

Kirsten scrambled to her feet and tried to hobble. Emma had grabbed Brandon by the shirt and was pulling him back. "Stop it!" she cried. "Control yourself, Brandon!"

Mole was just across the street. A small crowd stood out front, waiting to get in, and Kirsten limped as fast as she could into their midst. "Hey, are you okay?" the bouncer asked.

"I could use some ice," Kirsten replied.

He let her in and signaled to the bartender. The club was smaller than Cuts, with an air-conditioning system jacked up way too high, professional dancers in G-strings and little else on raised platforms, and couples—mainly same-sex but a little of everything—going at it on the dance floor. A retro mirror ball turned slowly, sending pinpricks of light around the room, and Kirsten limped to the bar, grimacing. Someday she'd sue Brandon.

The bartender, a blond woman, filled a sturdy plastic bag with ice and gave it to Kirsten. "What do you want to drink?" she asked.

"This is fine," Kirsten said, placing the bag on her ankle. "Actually, I'm looking for someone. . . ."

She gave the bartender a description of the red-haired guy, and of Sam, but got the same reaction she'd gotten all night: a blank look.

The numbing cold felt good. Kirsten glanced back to the door, afraid that Brandon may have come in, but he wasn't there.

On the stool next to her, a hunky jock-type guy with a slightly whirly-eyed, just-at-the-verge-of-too-drunk look on his face smiled at her and said in a deep voice, "Standard opening line."

"Excuse me?" Kirsten replied.

"Practiced confident reaction to affect attraction in a desirable member of the opposite sex." The guy laughed. "Sorry. It's a meta-conversation—like, a description of the underlying *meaning* of a conversation, instead of the actual words."

"Oh," Kirsten said. "Pretty geeky."

"Self-deprecating laugh with the realization that because contact has been established, the line has actually accomplished what it was meant to do." He grinned.

"Uh, sorry, I can't play the game. My ankle hurts, I've had a terrible night, I'm about to go home, and I'm just not smart enough. You must be at Columbia or something."

"A couple of miles to the south." He burped. "I'm at NYU Law now. But don't hold that against me—the burp or the college. I'm Chip, by the way—"

"Okay, Chip by the way, I have a question. I'm not supposed to be asking this. I'm supposed to be heading home, but I might as well ask you, anyway. You know the girl in the news reports? Samantha? Well, she's my friend and I'm trying to find her. She was last seen with this red-haired guy. They gave a police sketch on TV, but—"

"It sucked. Didn't look a thing like him, right?" Chip said.

Kirsten wasn't expecting *that*. "Yeah. That's right. . . ."

"I know the dude. Scruffy red hair, Phish

head, good looking, likes to barhop on the Upper East Side. You wouldn't tell it was him from that stupid-ass police composite, but yeah, couldn't be anyone else. I went to Andover with him, but I didn't know him well. He hung with the film crowd. Tim something or other."

"Tim?" Kirsten repeated.

"I'm pretty sure," Chip said. "His picture is in my yearbook."

Kirsten sat upright. Suddenly her ankle wasn't hurting so much anymore. "Do you still have it? The yearbook?"

"Sure. It's at my place."

What incredible luck! Kirsten looked him in the eye. He seemed pretty harmless. "'At my place'?" she said. "Standard come-on line to cute girl? Um, maybe you could go get your yearbook and bring it back? Pretty please?"

Chip laughed. "I live kind of far away. If I go and come back, thereby squandering a week's worth of personal spending money, how do I know you'll still be here? And if you're gone, it means I'll be stuck with a big-ass book full of pictures of prep school kids for the rest of the night. It's not exactly optimal for picking up a cute girl?"

"I can wait," Kirsten said with a smile. "My ankle is in lousy shape, anyway."

"Come with me," Chip said. "My roommates will be there. They never leave. They're engineering students. Even geekier than me."

Kirsten sighed. She'd promised Julie she'd be right home and wouldn't leave with anyone. She'd told Kyle she wouldn't do anything crazy. If she did this, she'd be breaking all her promises.

But if she didn't, she'd never see the photo. Never get Erik the Red's real name. Never come up with the lead that might get her closer to Sam. All for fear of a law student and his engineering roommates.

"I'll pay for the cab," Kirsten said.

"Only the lobby smells," Chip said, inserting his key in the front door of his building. "It's because of the restaurant next door."

Lobby was a pretty grand name for the miserable dingy cell they were in, with its broken black-and-white floor tiles and dented mailboxes on the wall. And any restaurant that

gave off such a god-awful stink had no business serving food to human beings. "So . . .
um, what neighborhood *is* this?" Kirsten
asked.

"I don't think there's a name for it," Chip
replied, "but it's walking distance to China-
town, Little Italy, SoHo, the East Village, the
Lower East Side."

"But not NYU . . ."

"A long walk." Chip grinned. "How do you
think I keep my boyish figure?"

From Kirsten's sense of the cab ride, anywhere would be a very long walk.

The door creaked open, and Chip held it for
her, which was a good thing because it looked
like it weighed about three tons, maybe 50
percent of that being old layers of paint.

Kirsten stepped into the building, and the
door swung shut with a loud *thwock* that
echoed up the shaft of the stairway. That was
about it for the public area—a longish hallway with graffiti-covered walls, three forebod-
ing metal doors, and a sturdy black industrial
stairway.

Chip's apartment was on the fifth floor.

He jammed another key into a door that

looked like it had been kicked in one too many times, and pushed it open. With a bow, he gestured Kirsten inside. "Welcome to my humble *château.*"

She'd read about "railroad flats" in books about New York, but this was the first she'd seen. The apartment was a string of small rooms; you had to go through each one to get to the next. A living room was at the end.

This was a very small railroad. It had that old-New-York-building smell of decay, which was like nothing else in the world—not exactly a food smell or a human smell, more like a faint cloud of highly concentrated dust, like the grime that collects on things kept in an attic for a few lifetimes.

They walked through door number one, the lone closet . . . door number two, empty kitchen . . . door number three, empty bedroom . . . and finally the living room. Also empty.

"Um . . . where is everybody?" Kirsten asked.

"Good question—they must be out," Chip said. Kirsten glanced around and began wondering exactly how many roommates there were in this very small place, and what kind of extra-close and kinky relationship they must have.

The living room décor was beer cans and empty chips and pretzels bags, CDs and magazines. The place was barely humanized by personal photos in plastic frames on the mantelpiece of a bricked-over fireplace.

Photos of Chip and various friends and family members.

Just Chip's family. Just Chip's friends.

"So how many roommates do you have?" Kirsten asked.

Chip was standing in the archway that led out of the apartment to the front door. He was smiling, but his expression had lost that half-drunk goofy geekiness it had in the bar and had turned into something else, something that did not make Kirsten feel all warm and snuggly inside.

With a heavy shrug he said, "Facial expression that translates as a sheepish admission of false pretenses."

Kirsten swallowed hard. "So . . . you lied? Is that what you're trying to tell me?"

"Okay, okay, let's end the game," Chip said.

"I have to admit something, Kirsten. I know Sam. I didn't tell you in the bar because I thought you'd freak out—big time."

"Really? You *know* Sam—*and* you know this Tim guy? Do you know where they are?"

Chip leaned against the side of the archway, looking absently at his nails. "I wonder if *you* know Sam as well as you think you do. She's into some, um, wild things. Things you don't know about. I used to see her at a bar way over on Fourteenth, a place called the Leather Vault. Weird crowd there . . . really weird . . . but kind of cool at the same time."

Great, Kirsten, just great, she thought angrily. *You've gotten yourself inside the apartment of a very strange, very large man in the middle of Manhattan's only neighborhood without a name, and he's telling you your best friend hangs out at S&M bars with an Andover guy named Tim who likes Phish and oh, by the way, the only way out is through this doorframe AND HE'S BLOCKING IT!*

It wasn't going to work. He was lying. "Where's the yearbook?" Kirsten asked. "Just show it to me, let me write down this guy's name, and then I'll get myself a cab, okay?"

"Oh, the yearbook . . ." Chip made a half-assed show of looking around the room. "I can't seem to locate it in my personal library. It must have been stolen." He pushed himself away from the archway, eyes locked on Kirsten's, and began walking steadily toward her. "Oh well, I guess we'll just have to think of something else to do."

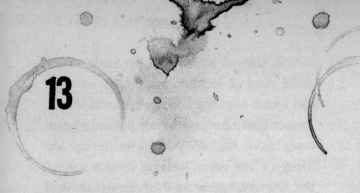

13

The window?

No. Too high up.

Scream?

Who would give a shit in this neighborhood?

Call the police?

Her cell was dead, and there was no way she could ever find his phone. There was nothing 'real' in this shithole of an apartment.

"You told me it was here, Chip." Kirsten backed away, stepping on things that crackled and crunched, but there was no place to back to. She was against the wall. "You told me you had roommates and that you went to Andover."

"You didn't come all the way here to look at a yearbook, Kirsten," Chip said. "You came because you wanted to."

She could feel his breath now. And his eyes,

burning down the front of her like a laser. His hand reached around and grabbed the left side of her butt.

No time to think. She reared back with her right leg, as far as she could, and let loose a sharp knee to the balls.

"Aaaaaggghhhhhhh!" Chip doubled over in pain.

Kirsten shoved him aside and ran. She could hear him fall into a pile of debris, moaning loudly.

The front door was stuck. No, bolted. Three times.

She twisted and untwisted, the tumblers on the locks clicking wildly before the door suddenly shot open and she nearly fell into the stairwell.

A surprised rodent, or maybe an industrial-grade insect, scurried for cover as Kirsten pounded down the stairs. He would recover. He would come after her. How long did it take guys to recover from something like this? Long enough for her to get a cab?

Fourth floor. Doors opening, frightened eyes peering out from cracks, behind small chains.

Third floor. Second floor. Despite her bad ankle, Kirsten jumped half of the last flight and landed in a heap on the ground level. Scrambling to her feet, she body-slammed the ancient outer door and bolted out onto the street.

Chip's building was mid-block, and to the left, a gang of seedy-looking guys lurked on the corner, talking loudly into cell phones.

Not there. She turned and ran the other way, without looking, because there was no time for that, and after two steps collided with someone she hadn't seen.

"Ahhhhhh!" she screamed, and instinctively grabbed his arm, wrenching it hard behind his back. "Leave me alone, you asshole!"

"Ow! Kirsten, it's me. Let go! Please!"

It wasn't Chip. Not at all.

"*Kyle?* Oh, my God, Kyle, what are you doing here?" Kristen asked, releasing him from her death grip.

"Well, I, um, actually—," he stammered.

There was no time. Not here. Not within sight of Chip's apartment.

Kirsten grabbed his hand. "Come on!"

She ran to the next street, pulling Kyle behind her. There were no cabs there or anywhere. A row of metal-gated shops lined both sides of the deserted street, a boarded-up old theater at the end of the block.

They ran to the theater and ducked into the dark alcove under the old marquee. They weren't alone, but the other people were fast asleep under ratty blankets against the door.

"Sorry . . . Kirsten . . . ," Kyle said, catching his breath. "I didn't mean to scare you—I was following you, but I lost track. . . ."

"Following me?" Kirsten said. "Really? Like, *all night?*" She wasn't sure how to react.

"Well, yeah . . . more or less . . . ," he said.

Kirsten was stunned. She'd been out for hours. What had he been doing? Had he been in the clubs? Walking behind her and Julie on the sidewalks? Tailing her in cabs? It was strange. It was *spying*.

"You could have said hello," she said, but she hated the words the moment they came out of her mouth. "I mean, don't get me wrong, Kyle, I'm *so* grateful you're here now— I don't know what I would have done without you—but still . . . following me? *All night?*"

"It was dumb, I know," Kyle said sheepishly. "I just—well, after our conversation in Jackson Hole, I thought you might be headed for trouble. I figured you'd get mad if you saw me, so I kind of stayed low. I missed you when you left Cuts, but heard the fight with Brandon, only by the time I got there, you'd run into Mole. Anyway, I waited outside and jumped in a cab when you took off with that guy. But we lost track of you—the driver didn't know this neighborhood too well—so I've been kind of wandering around, hoping I'd see you. I'm really, really glad I did." He looked at his feet.

Kirsten let out a sigh. He was worried about her, that's all. Actually, when she thought about it, what he did was kind of nice. "I guess I'm glad you found me, too, Kyle," she admitted. "Next time I do something like this, I'll take you along. Okay?"

"Next time?" Kyle asked. "You plan on doing this a lot?"

Kirsten smiled. "Depends on the company."

Kyle leaned close, and all the feelings that had built up over the night—the fear and anger, frustration and betrayal—began to lift, leaving Kirsten feeling cold and fragile and empty and sad.

She needed a hug. Badly. She threw her arms around Kyle, letting go of the last remnants of the night's sleaze and terror, and she held tightly until her cheeks rested in a warm patch of her tears on his shoulder. "It's my fault, Kyle. You warned me, but I ignored you. I thought I could find her. I thought if I didn't try, no one else would. I was so stupid! And I let this . . . this creep trick me. . . ."

Kyle folded her in his arms. "Hey, it's all right. . . . You're safe. . . . You don't have to explain."

They stood there, saying nothing, rocking back and forth, until Kirsten was feeling calmer, and he seemed to sense the moment it was all right to move. Together they walked to a wide, two-way street—Delancey—and flagged down a livery cab driver.

And after a bumpy cross-town ride, they were gliding up the West Side Highway, the black sash of the Hudson River to their left, reflecting the moon and the bright thickets of lights from the high-rises in New Jersey.

Kyle lived on 112th and Morningside, a quiet street on the *way* Upper West Side, near Columbia University. They got out at a dark brownstone on a quiet block.

"Your parents live here?" Kirsten asked.

"No, a friend," he said. "A senior at Columbia. It's student housing. He's letting me crash."

"When do you go have to go back to Maine?" Kirsten asked.

"Shhh. Don't worry about that." Kyle let her into the building and showed her to a small, first-floor apartment with a smudged Quik-Erase notepad on the door and furnished with exactly two chairs and a ripped sofa, a TV, a sound system, and a card table. He made cocoa on a hot plate while she sat on the sofa under a soft cotton blanket that he had pulled off a chair.

It was cold and cheaply furnished, and there was dust all over the place, but Kirsten felt absolutely divine.

Kyle put on a slow, sleepy jazz CD and kneeled on the floor close to her, next to the sofa. Close enough so that Kirsten knew exactly how she felt inside, that for the first time tonight, for the first time in a long time, there was nothing to worry about, nothing to hold her back. And the shudder of guilt and sadness, the thought of Sam and where she might be at that moment, gave way to a voice in her head that was part Sam's too, that said being here with Kyle was the right thing to do.

"Are you all right?" Kyle asked, tenderly sweeping her hair away from her face.

She rested her head on his shoulder, closed her eyes, breathed the fading scent of his cologne, and finally relaxed.

When he kissed her, she pulled him gently onto the sofa and knew by his touch that the night, as far as she was concerned, was going to be just fine.

She awoke to the sound of an ambulance screaming by.

Kyle's eyes flickered open. They were still on the sofa, wrapped in his blanket, and when he moved away, the cold rushed in to chill the warmth their bodies had created. "Sorry about that. The hospital is a block away."

Kirsten looked at the clock on the wall. It was 4:07 A.M. "Oh, my God," she said, jumping off the couch and retrieving her things from the floor. "My parents, at the moment, probably think I'm the next Paris Hilton and are ready to kill me."

"I'd better get you a cab." Kyle stood up, reaching for a long-sleeved tee that was hanging over the side of a chair.

A big Grover from *Sesame Street* was printed on it.

Kirsten laughed. "Wearing *that?*"

"If you don't love Grover," Kyle said, pulling the shirt down over his head, "then I'm sorry, there's no future for us!"

They hurried out onto the street, which was absolutely silent and beautiful. Kirsten rested her head against Kyle's shoulder until they reached Broadway, where she prayed there were no cabs, which would force them to go back until the morning—but this was New York, and a taxi pulled up right away.

"Bye," Kirsten said.

Kyle opened the door her, and she stepped inside.

And she discovered that even after a night like she'd just had, a simple kiss on the street from a twenty-one-year-old guy in a Grover shirt could rock her world.

* * *

"Hey, lady, the meter's runnin'."

When those romantic words awoke her fifteen minutes later, she was sprawled out in the backseat of the taxi. The driver, leaning over the front seat, had the hairiest nostrils she had ever seen.

She gave him a twenty and told him to keep the change, and the guy nearly knocked over Hector in a race to open the cab's back door for her.

She floated into the building, her permagrin practically blinding herself in the elevator mirror. She knew there were going to be frantic, angry messages on her cell, couldn't check now anyway. She'd get the lecture soon enough, and she figured she'd hang on to the good mood while she could.

Quickly she took off her shoes. Chances were that Mom and Dad had gone to bed, and she could tiptoe into her room unnoticed.

Ding. The door whooshed open into the penthouse.

Kirsten cautiously stepped in, taking care to avoid the floorboard that always creaked.

"Hi, sweetie," came Mom's voice from the kitchen.

Shit, Kirsten thought.

They were waiting, both of them fully dressed and standing at the archway from the foyer to the kitchen. But they didn't look angry.

Mom's makeup was gone, her skin pale and puffy. Dad's eyes were red, and his mouth drawn in a tight line trying so desperately to be neutral looking that it scared Kirsten. She felt her knees weaken, and she sat on a wooden banquet seat in the foyer. "You have something to tell me . . . ," she said, not wanting to hear it, but knowing that she had to.

Her parents both pulled up chairs from the kitchen and sat close to her, facing her. And she knew exactly what they were going to say before it came out of their mouths. But until the last second she hoped, hoped she wrong, and they were merely going to yell at her, scream at her, *disown* her, any of which would have been fine, anything else but the words that now came haltingly, half-choked, out of her father's mouth.

"Kirsten, I . . . I don't know how to tell you this," he said, "but . . . Sam is dead."

Part Two

Part One

14

Dead.

Sam was dead.

The reality hit her over and over, through the night, through the sunrise she hadn't even noticed—the image of Sam promising to call, the scream that was erased by mistake, the look on her mom's face the night before, the awful news . . .

It always came back to that night at the Party Room, to one simple truth.

Sam was never coming home. *Why didn't I stop her?* Kirsten asked herself. *Why didn't I force her to stay with us that night?*

When the smell of coffee and bacon wafted into her darkened room from the kitchen, Kirsten realized it was morning. The hours of crying had wrung her dry. Her lips were parched, her body achy.

Slipping on her robe and mules, she shuffled

out of her room for some water. In the kitchen, Dad was eating his breakfast alone, already dressed in an elegant gray suit and starched white shirt, as usual, but looking haggard and old. In the background, Sandy Kenyon of WINS radio was delivering the day's celebrity Hollywood news, usually Kirsten's favorite feature, but she wasn't hearing a word, and instead of listening went straight to the fridge to pour herself a glass of bottled water. "They've been talking about Sam all morning," Dad said grimly. "Nonstop."

Kirsten wasn't interested. She grunted an "Oh" and began heading back to her room, when the radio let out a blast like a symphony orchestra, and an urgent voice intoned, *"We bring you the latest on the breaking story of the Samantha Byrne Murder case. . . ."*

Murder.

Kirsten sank into a kitchen chair, feeling short of breath.

". . . In what seems like a grotesque reenactment of a three-year-old news story, a senior from a prestigious New York City private school was found bludgeoned to death in Central Park, in nearly the same location—and by exactly the

same method as the infamous Talcott murder three years ago. Samantha Byrne, whose disappearance was reported by her parents after what was by all accounts a typical night of wild partying on the Upper East Side, was found today by an early-morning jogger. Authorities say the teenager was stabbed over seventy times, then beat repeatedly in the right temporal lobe. Her mouth was found to be gagged with newspaper, and her hands were bound with a tie—a tie decorated with the symbol of Talcott Preparatory School. . . ."

"Oh my God . . . ," Kirsten whispered. "Oh, my God . . ."

"For New Yorkers, the murder recalls that of Carolee Adams, whose convicted killer, Paul Stone, was released earlier this year on a legal technicality. Stone had always maintained his innocence and has not been seen since. . . ."

Kirsten couldn't listen. Forgetting her water, she ran into her room and stood by the window, staring over the trees, over the gray-blue expanse of the Reservoir in the park.

Where had it happened? Right outside her room? Had Sam been there, crying for help, when Kirsten arrived home Friday night?

Where was the yellow police tape? She didn't see any police tape.

It wasn't true. It couldn't be.

Kirsten tried to remember the details of the Carolee Adams case, but it was all a blur now. She was just fourteen when it'd happened, entering high school, meeting new friends and having fun. At that time, she didn't know Carolee or any of the kids at Talcott. The murder was something so far removed from her life. She never thought it would affect her directly . . . that is, until now.

After Carolee was killed, Paul Stone's photo had appeared in all the papers. Kirsten wished she remembered what he looked like—but she had only a vague recollection: blondish hair, bland expression. She wasn't even sure of that.

And now he was free. *They let him off.* But people who did those kinds of things usually came back to do them again. Everyone knew that. How could they have let him go?

Kirsten pulled her curtains shut, nearly ripping them from their hooks, blocking the view she never wanted to see again. And she collapsed on the bed, feeling sick and hollow.

She wasn't aware of dozing off, but the sharp rapping on her door roused her from an agitated sleep.

The door opened, and Julie, Sarah, and Carla peered in. They all looked like shit, and they didn't say a word, just ran in and wrapped Kirsten in a big, communal, tearful hug that broke through the numbness.

Kirsten held them tight and cried. She couldn't say a word, couldn't bear to believe that the circle of friends had shrunk forever. There were four of them now. All her life there had been five. The playdates, the birthday parties, the homework sessions and all-night IMing—*five*. It had never occurred to her that it would ever be different.

"School was canceled," Julie finally said, her face pink and swollen. "Your mom called our parents and invited us over to keep you company. I—I just can't believe it, Kirsten."

"What are we going to do?" Kirsten said. "How can she be gone?"

"And *murdered*," Carla said, shaking her head. "It doesn't seem possible. . . ."

"I remember when they let that guy out of jail," Sarah said. "I knew something bad would happen. I had a feeling. But who would have thought . . . ?"

A Talcott tie. That was what stuck in Kirsten's mind. Talcott was one of the most prestigious schools in the East. She had a sudden realization. "Wait. Didn't Brandon go to Talcott?"

Carla nodded. "He transferred to Woodley freshman year."

"Right after the murder," Julie added.

"He never talks about it," Carla said. "The only time I ever heard him mention Talcott was in the Party Room, when someone else brought it up in conversation. Brandon got all weird. Said he hated the place, didn't have any friends there, didn't even like to think about it. Makes you wonder."

"Oh my God, oh my God . . . ," Sarah murmured.

"I don't know," Julie said. "He is a slimeball, but it doesn't mean he's a . . ."

Murderer?

Kirsten filled in the rest of the sentence, but her mind was racing back . . .

To the night before, when Brandon was following her across Little Twelfth Street. To his explosion at the Party Room on Friday night, and his threats on Madison Avenue. To the day he'd backed her against the wall, outside of school. She could still hear the words he'd said as if he were there:

I'm going to trash your life. And when you least expect it, when everything seems to be going your way, you're going to pay. . . .

When he was on drugs, Brandon was capable of anything. Could he have done it?

Kirsten felt tears welling up again at the thought. What did it matter? Sam was gone. Nothing would bring her back.

But if Brandon laid a hand on her, if he was the one, Kirsten wanted to know. Because he would be the one to pay.

Kirsten buttoned her Burberry jacket against the suddenly sharp wind that evening as she rounded the corner of Eighty-third and First with her friends.

It had been the longest day of her life. She hadn't eaten when her friends were over. She hadn't eaten after they'd left. She'd tried Kyle on his cell all day but only got voice mail. Mom and Dad were sweet, staying home and holding her and crying with her and getting her to drink tea. But the phone kept ringing all day. Finally she mustered up the energy to go over to Sam's mom's place, which was just the worst. Everyone wanted to rehash and console and cry. And throughout all of it, *Peterson,* bugging her at least five times for more information, all the while insisting that she *mustn't* think it was her fault, which was the most ridiculous thing to say, *because at a time like this, who was thinking about fault?*

Okay, she was. All the time, every minute. How easy it would have been to have pulled Sam back into the Party Room when she was on her way out . . . or earlier, when they'd first walked in and seen Brandon, to have suggested a different bar. Either way, and with a hundred other scenarios, none of this would have happened. And somehow, who knows how it happened, in the middle of all that, she'd somehow agreed with the girls to come to the Party Room, which at the moment seemed like the world's worst idea ever.

Kirsten paused, her knees shaking, as they approached the familiar oak door to their favorite haunt. "Guys, this is really, really stupid. Why are we doing this?"

Julie stopped and turned to Kirsten, taking both her arms and looking her firmly in the eye. "We talked about this, Kirsten, and we all agreed. We've been home all day. We're going to be home tonight and all day tomorrow. The phones, the media, the crying—it's too much. We love Sam, Kirsten. We want to honor *her,* not everybody else's take on her story, everyone else wanting to analyze and figure it out for their own mind. *This* is what Sam would have wanted, Kirsten. Not for us to sit around and cry. For us to *do* something—something crazy and fun."

"But the memory . . . ," Kirsten said. "It was only five nights ago. . . ."

"Think about the other memories," Sarah said. "All the nights we spent with her here."

"This place *was* Sam," Julie reminded her. "Her soul is still here."

Kirsten took a deep breath. She tried to imagine what Sam would say if she were here—if she were hovering around watching her friends react to her death. She would nod and sympathize. She would be touched that they all loved her so much. But then, after a while, she would smile and push them right through this door. And she would say, *Have one on me.* "Yeah," Kirsten said. "Let's go."

As the girls descended the staircase, the bouncers nodded solemnly. The music was loud, the floor pretty sparse. Not a big Woodley crowd tonight, although members of some of the other classes were here, people who didn't know Sam.

Kirsten was not up for dancing. Not yet. She needed a drink.

Scott was dressed in black, but he was always in black. "Hey," he said gently, "how are you guys holding up?"

Kirsten tried to smile. "I could use some help."

"It's on me," Scott said, sliding a drink across the bar to her. "I've got my eye out for Red. The minute he shows his face in here, he's toast."

Red. Kirsten had thought about him a lot today too. Could he be Paul Stone with his hair dyed? He was probably about the right age. But when she imagined Scott—or Peterson, or anybody—catching Red, it didn't make her feel better. Having Sam back would make her feel better. "I just can't believe this really happened. Why? Why *Sam?*"

Scott sighed. "I've seen so much shit in my life. You never think it's going to happen to you. Never. But the world has a way of knocking you on your ass when you least expect it, and you just have no control."

"But I could have *done* something, Scott!" Kirsten said.

"What? Run over and blocked the door? Pushed her back into the bar? She was a big girl, Kirsten. She had her own mind." Scott put his hand gently on Kirsten's shoulder. "You shouldn't have done anything different. You did what a good friend does. Look at me, Kirsten. *It's not your fault.*"

Kirsten nodded. Out of the corner of her eye, she spotted Emma Lewis floating like a zombie through the sparse crowd. Her hair was limp and unbrushed, her eyes red, her Sam-like makeup all gone.

"Sorry, Scott . . . I'm out of here," Kirsten said, pushing back her barstool.

But she wasn't fast enough. Emma stood in front of her, cornering her between the stools and the bar. "Oh, Kirsten. I—I feel soooo guilty. So totally guilty. Oh, my God. Can you ever . . ." Her voice broke, and she began to sob, the words barely escaping from her mouth. "Can . . . you ever . . . forgive me?"

"You're forgiven, Emma," Kirsten said, rolling her eyes. She was not in the mood for this drama. "For whatever. Now would you leave me alone?"

"You don't understand!" Emma blurted out, choking back tears. "I—I *did it. I'm the one who did it!*"

15

Emma was sobbing, the words caught in her throat, and Kirsten had to force herself to breathe because the thought of what Emma was trying to say, the implication in all its bizarreness, was catching her off-guard. "What, Emma? What are you talking about? *Tell me exactly what you did!*"

Julie, Carla, and Sarah, who had been dancing listlessly, came running.

"I'm s-sorry . . ." Emma nodded, gulping hysterically. "It started as a game, but I didn't realize—it's a crime, a serious crime—"

Kirsten held on to Julie, who was stiff, uncomprehending. "Oh, Emma . . . oh, God, don't tell me this . . ."

"I—I didn't even think I was capable of doing it! I learned how to change the Reply-to address. Josh Bergen showed me. It wasn't Sam. *I'm sooooo sorry.* Will you ever forgive me?"

Kirsten let go of Julie, and her knees nearly buckled. "*The e-mail*—is that what you're telling me? You wrote that stupid bogus-sounding e-mail? Is that *all?*"

"Emma, you scared the shit out of us!" Carla said.

"I don't really know why I did it," Emma barged on. "At the time . . . I was convinced Sam was all right. And Kirsten, you had been so upset when I saw you on Woodley Hill. I wanted you to feel better. So . . . I sent the message. I know it was totally crazy. If I had known . . ."

Kirsten leaned against the bar. "Get out of here, Emma. You're really sick."

"I can't believe she's really dead, Kirsten," Emma said. "I've been crying all day, watching the news. Brandon's upset too. I went to his house—you know, to comfort him—I mean, he's the only one who loved Sam as much as you and I did—"

"Brandon never loved Sam," Kirsten snapped.

"You should have seen him. He was acting *so* weird—totally freaked out. Saying all kinds of stuff, not making any sense. He wouldn't even come out of his house! He scared me so much." Her hands trembling, Emma lowered her voice.

Julie, Carla, and Sarah moved in closer.

"I saw something . . . at his house . . . ," Emma said, "something that scared me. I mean, it may not mean anything, so I don't want to say it. . . ."

"What?" Julie insisted. "What are you talking about?"

"Brandon keeps a Talcott tie pinned to a dartboard in his room," Emma whispered. "Today the tie was missing."

Oh, God. Kirsten closed her eyes as her mind whirred. Suddenly things were beginning to connect. Brandon was a Talcott student three years ago—when Carolee was killed. And the guy they put in jail, Stone, no one really knew if he'd done it. He was released and there *had* to be a reason for that—which meant that the killer would still be out there. . . .

Was it possible? Kirsten wondered. No, it was a crazy idea. Brandon was only fourteen back then, and why would he do it? Why?

But she *did* know why he might want to

hurt Sam. Maybe even . . . kill her?

"The moment I brought it up," Emma went on, "he told me to get out."

Kirsten shared a look with her friends. Whether Brandon was a murderer or not, it was clear that he was unstable and dangerous.

"Emma, does he know you're here?" Carla asked.

Emma nodded. "I'm worried."

"Stay away from him," Kirsten said. "Don't let him know that you told us. You'll have to tell Detective Peterson about this."

"Help me, Kirsten," Emma said, tears falling down her cheeks. "I'm scared. He's mad at me now. What if he . . . ?" Her voice trailed off as she nervously pushed her hair back behind her ears.

Kirsten noticed that her earrings were off and her bracelet was missing. "Emma, what happened to your jewelry?"

Emma stiffened. "It's at home. Why?"

"You've been wearing it every day."

"It—it reminds me of Sam. It makes me sad, Kirsten. Why do you ask?"

Kirsten didn't know the answer. Except

that it seemed strange. It just seemed strange. "You're not trying to be Sam anymore—why, Emma? *Why aren't you trying to be like Sam?*"

"Kirsten . . . you're scaring me . . . ," Emma said. "Sam is dead. I don't want to be like Sam anymore! You can't make me!"

Scaring *her?* Kirsten couldn't imagine *anyone* being more frightened than she was—or more confused. And for once she didn't think that her friends could help her sort this whole thing out. She needed to talk to Kyle—now. "You know what? It really wasn't a good idea for me to come here. I've got to go."

"But we just got here," Julie said.

"I know, but I'm not feeling well." Kirsten was walking fast now, practically jogging to the door.

"Where are you going to be?" Carla called out.

Kirsten put her hand to her ear, thumb and pinkie outstretched. "I'll call," she said, before running through the door.

And her stomach did a flip-flop. That was Sam's exact gesture, on her way out of the Party Room Friday night. On the way to her death.

Kirsten bolted upstairs and caught a cab to the Upper West Side. On the way, she tried Kyle at least ten times on the cell, but just got his message.

The taxi dropped her off at Kyle's West 112th Street apartment, and Kirsten saw that the light in the first-floor apartment was off.

Fine. She would wait. He had to show up sometime.

Some of the apartment windows were open, and from the floors above, it seemed as if Eminem were trying to outshout Missy Elliot.

She walked up the stoop and pressed the buzzer.

A college kid, wearing headphones and dressed in head-to-toe Fubu, came barreling through the door. He held it open, releasing a smell of frying burgers and burnt tomato sauce.

"Thanks," Kirsten said to him.

"I'm in 3C, babe," the guy said as he left, not giving Kirsten the chance to kick his ass.

Okay, so maybe I won't wait for Kyle in the building. I could write him a note and hang out at the corner Starbucks. There has to be a corner Starbucks around here somewhere, she thought, rushing up to Kyle's apartment. She reached for the Quik-Erase notepad—and noticed that the door was ajar.

"Kyle?" she called, pushing it open wide.

Her voice echoed eerily in the dark, and she fumbled for the light switch.

Click. The light came on. And Kirsten let out a gasp.

The chairs, the ripped couch, the sound system, and CDs—all were gone.

She ran into the kitchen alcove and pulled open the cabinets, checking each one for signs of life. Nothing. Not even a single macaroni-and-cheese package.

Then she rushed to the bedroom and pulled open the closet—only to find a bunch of old wire hangers inside. That's it.

The apartment was empty.

And Kyle was gone.

16

Kirsten's mind raced.

Kyle's friend was a student. Maybe his semester was over. Maybe he was kicked out of school and had to leave right away—and so did Kyle?

She heard the clatter of footsteps in the hall and ran to the door, startling another guy, this one dressed top-to-toe in crisp Abercrombie and Fitch.

"Did you see what happened here?" she asked.

The guy peered into the room. "Whoa . . . so *that's* what all the noise was about. Guess the dude moved out."

"Did you know him?" Kirsten asked.

"Nope. Kept to himself." He leaned against the doorjamb and smiled. "That sucks. You have no date tonight, huh?"

Kirsten barged past him and ran out of the

building. She pulled a stick of gum from her backpack and popped it into her mouth, chewing nervously. Head down, she headed for Broadway.

There had to be an explanation. People didn't just vanish. *He'll call,* she told herself. *He probably spent the day moving. Maybe his cell died and he couldn't get to a pay phone. It's not his fault. He'll apologize and invite me to his new place.* She checked her cell again. No messages.

At the corner of 112th and Broadway, Kirsten tossed her gum wrapper into the trash. It slid down the front page of a discarded *New York Post,* neatly folded over, which had a headline so huge and hysterical, you could practically hear it screaming.

DID TALCOTT KILLER KILL AGAIN?

Under the headline, just above the fold, was a photo—the top of someone's head. Kirsten gave the paper a quick once-over for banana peels and spit, but it was spotless, so she carefully fished it out and let it drop open.

It was a mug shot. A face staring directly

into the camera, almost defiantly, eyes half-lidded. His hair, kinky and blond, was piled thickly on his head, and his scraggly beard hung from his chin like wet moss.

She caught a glimpse of the caption: PAUL STONE.

She remembered him now. How the newspapers and TV reporters had always described him as a bland-looking guy, totally nondescript.

But it wasn't true. It was just the expression on his face—dull and lifeless. Under those drugged-out lids his eyes were dark and piercing, and the beard obscured a jaw that was clearly fine-boned and chiseled. If you imagined the beard gone, the hair tamed, the eyes wide open, and some weight loss, he wouldn't be half bad looking.

It took a few seconds to sink in before she realized something else. Something important.

She knew Paul Stone.

She knew exactly who he was.

"Oh my God . . ." Kirsten's hand shook. She had to balance the newspaper on the rim of the trashcan, just to read the article.

NEW YORK, LATE EDITION—
New York City's declining crime rate may have its mayor bragging about "the safest city on earth," but don't tell that to the students of the prestigious Woodley School in Riverdale—or to their parents. "Letting Paul Stone out of jail was a travesty of justice," said Dr. Richard Fenk, plastic surgeon and father of a Woodley senior. "He should be in jail for life. And now the bastard is out—scot-free. As a father, what am I supposed to do now—keep my daughter under lock and key?"

On a blustery fall day, when Woodley would normally be filled with the chatter of teens comparing notes, fashions, and fancy vacations, the school was vacant. Three blocks away, the victim's mother, socialite Barbara "Bobbi" Knauerhase, formerly Byrne, waved reporters away as she left her luxurious Park Avenue apartment, too distressed to talk. Her husband, personal trainer Rolf Knauerhase, vowed that "this sub-human piece of garbage will soon be crushed."

Rumors have been circulating that Stone, now 21, has adopted a new identity—perhaps, speculates Dr. Fenk, with the aid of plastic surgery. According to a spokesman for the New York City Police Department, Detective Norman "Pete" Peterson . . .

Kirsten couldn't continue with the article. The photo kept staring at her. Daring her to look. It was the face of a killer.

She aged the face in her mind, colored the hair brown, imagined it calm and happy and smiling. At first glance, no, it wouldn't have been obvious. But it was clear when you knew what you were looking at.

The shape, the tilt of the head, the slightly forward slant of the forehead—it had to be him.

But it couldn't be him.

She held on to a slim hope, that there might be something—a scar, a birthmark, a crossed eye—something that would give away the fact that they were different people.

But the more she looked at it, the more obvious it became.

Leslie's dad was wrong. Paul Stone hadn't had plastic surgery.

A razor. Dye. Age. That was all he'd used.

A new identity.

Kyle had never told her his last name. Never mentioned much about his past.

But now it made sense.

Paul was Kyle.

Kyle was Paul.

Kirsten was in love with a murderer.

Sam's murderer.

From the depths of the night she heard a muffled howl. Only when people began to stare did she realize it was coming from her own throat.

17

Kirsten wasn't sure how she made it home to the familiar confines of the Upper East Side. One minute she was sick, hovered over a city garbage can accepting a crumpled napkin from some homeless woman so she could wipe her mouth. Then, as if by magic, she found herself climbing the familiar steps of the Metropolitan Museum of Art.

She slumped in the darkness next to one of the museum's old fountains and glanced at her watch. Three hours. She had been walking the city for three hours, thinking about her best friend's murder. Thinking about how it might have happened. How scared Sam must have been when she'd realized it was all about to end—right before her skull was cracked open.

Kirsten shuddered, imagining Sam's last few minutes of torment. And it had all happened practically right outside Kirsten's bedroom window—in the park where their nannies had taken them every day as kids, the place where she and Sam would sneak away to smoke cigarettes and talk about boys and about their dreams for the future. They were supposed to share an apartment in TriBeCa and go to NYU and after they graduated they had planned to spend a few years living in Florence so they could drive the Italian boys wild and go a little crazy themselves before they finally decided to get serious about their careers.

But now Sam was dead.

And then there was her murderer. Kyle . . . or Paul . . . or whatever his name was.

Kirsten's stomach lurched when she remembered their tender night together, how happy and giddy she was . . . how she didn't want to leave him, that night or ever. She closed her eyes, and the image of his cold, blank mug shot appeared before her. *Did he know I was Sam's friend before he'd even met me? He said he wanted to help me find Sam's killer. Was it all part of some weird, disgusting plan? How could I have been so stupid?*

"This whole thing is sick!" she screamed, not caring if the socialites out for an evening stroll with their overmanicured puppies thought she was crazy. She let the tears stream from her eyes. She let all of her emotions bubble to the surface.

Finally, Kirsten took a deep breath and decided to head to her apartment across the street, her only solace that now she knew the truth and that she'd tell the police about Paul Stone first thing in the morning.

On the corner of Eighty-second she saw the shadow of a man slumped against a building, homeless and poor, and it struck her that on the other side of the wall of that building, *her* building, was someone else living in the midst of the greatest wealth per square foot in the country. She had the urge to give the guy everything she had. She reached into her pocket, fumbling for cash. "Here," said Kirsten, holding out a fistful of bills. "Take this."

He reached out, and his face came into the light. "Kirsten—"

Kirsten froze and stared at the face of Sam's killer, his eyes shadowed by a long-brimmed baseball cap. "Kyle," she said, wanting to run but too scared to move.

"I've been waiting for you." He stepped forward and pulled her into an embrace.

He doesn't know that I know, Kirsten realized. Her stomach churning, she forced herself to hug him back. But it wasn't the same, and Kyle noticed.

"Hey, what's wrong?" he asked, pulling away. "Have you been crying?"

Kirsten didn't want to talk. She just wanted to get out of there. She glanced at her building's entrance at the center of the block. "I—I've got to go," she said, starting for the door.

"No—wait," Kyle said, gripping her wrist tightly. "We have to talk." He started pulling her in the opposite direction. "I've got something . . . important to tell you. It's kind of about Sam."

Kirsten began to panic. It was just like every thriller movie she'd ever seen. First, the killer explains how he murdered your best friend. Then, he murders *you* because you know too much! "No!" she said. "No, please!"

"Shhhhhh!" Kyle pushed his right hand over

her mouth and pulled her back . . . back . . . down the street and into a darkened service entrance.

She kicked and fought to get away. But Kyle was just too strong. With one arm he turned her around and pinned her to the door. And then she saw it—a Talcott tie dangling from his hand! "No, please. Don't kill me. Don't kill me!" she cried.

18

"What? No...Kirsten...
I wanted to show this to you. My Talcott tie."
Kyle loosened his grip on her.

"So what?" Kirsten said. "Anybody could buy a Talcott tie. It proves nothing."

From above, a window opened. *"Hey, what's going on down there?"*

Mr. Federman—the celebrity defense lawyer and the father of Frankie, who was the likely candidate for Woodley valedictorian. One word to him, and the police would appear instantly.

"Kirsten, you don't understand," Kyle whispered, breathing heavily. "I have a tie, but that doesn't make me a murderer. You're right. It's so easy to get one of these ties. I didn't kill anybody. You have to believe me."

"How can I?" Kirsten said. "You lied about your real name, *Paul.*"

"Please. Don't call me that," Kyle said softly. "Paul died when they locked me up. Those bastards ruined my name and destroyed my family."

"Do you kids know what time it is?" Mr. Federman yelled down. *"I'm calling the police!"*

Kyle's eyes burned through the darkness, steady and intense. He wasn't moving, wasn't running. "If you want to tell him, go ahead. If you want to leave, fine—but I've been in jail for two years for something I didn't do. That's why I came back—to clear my name so I can be free, have a normal life." His voice faltered, and he hesitated as if he wanted to say more but wasn't sure he should.

"What?" Kirsten said, trying to process it all. He sounded so sincere, so confused and hurt. "What did you want to say?"

"Just that when I met you . . . after all that's happened to me . . . you made me realize that I could still open up to people. I trust you, Kirsten. Please, try to trust me."

Kirsten looked away. *Trust?* The word ripped her apart. He was reaching inside her, right into her soul, to the place where she could be hurt the most. She wanted to trust him, but she wondered if that was part of the plan, too, if that was what he'd done to Sam and to Carolee.

When she looked back, she saw that he'd moved aside.

She stepped forward. She was on the sidewalk now. A few steps and she'd be around the corner, on Fifth Avenue.

Home.

She glanced up to Mr. Federman's open window. *"It's me, Mr. Federman, Kirsten Sawyer! Sorry about the noise. It's nothing. We'll be quiet, I promise!"*

The old man appeared at the window, dressed in a plaid nightshirt. With a nasty grumble, he slammed the window shut.

Kyle smiled. "Thanks."

"Look, I want to believe you," Kirsten said, "but how can I? You're not who you say you are. You disappear from your apartment without telling me—"

"I had to," he said. "My face is so familiar right now. I can't stay in one place very long."

"And the next place I see you is the front page of the *New York Post. You had a trial.* They convicted you, Kyle."

"I was released!" Kyle insisted.

"On a *technicality*," Kirsten reminded him, "whatever the hell *that* means."

"It means they had no grounds to arrest me in the first place. Inadmissible evidence. It means they nailed me for no reason. They convicted the wrong guy."

Kyle reached for her, but Kirsten stepped back. "I need proof, Kyle."

"Okay. The night Sam disappeared? I wasn't even in New York. I was in the Hamptons. I took the Jitney."

"Who were you staying with?"

"I was alone, Kirsten. At my parents' summer house. I have a key. They don't know I went. Nobody knows. That's my point. If they try to hang Sam's murder on me, I'm dead. I have no alibi. That's why I need you."

"Need *me?* For what? I wasn't there. What could I do?" Inside, she was so confused. Part of her wanted to hate him and turn him in—and the other part wanted to help him, somehow, to help him clear his name and feel once again the closeness they'd shared. She wanted to ride out tonight, escape with him and live cocooned in a cabin somewhere in the wilderness, sipping hot cocoa under warm blankets, far away from the city, the media, and murder. How could she want that, too? How?

"You have to vouch for me, Kirsten," Kyle said. "You have to tell them we were together that night. We were at my apartment, listening to CDs."

"But . . . but that's not true," Kirsten said.

"You could just say it was."

"You . . . want me to *lie* for you?"

"Not lie," Kyle pleaded, stepping toward her. "Just back me up, in case they come after me."

Kirsten stepped back.

No. That's not the way it worked. What was it Peterson had told her? *Lying for a friend is never a good idea. . . . You just get wrapped up in bigger and bigger lies. And before you know it, you're involved. . . .* "I can't, Kyle," she said.

"But Kirsten, it's the only way. . . ."

He was deluding himself, and she was deluding *herself* if she believed this would work. If Kyle was to clear his name, if he was going to fight lies and prove his innocence, he had to do it with truth. Otherwise, he was a bad bet for her, plain and simple. He'd be carrying around a whole web of lies that would just continue to grow. And that's if he was innocent.

If he was guilty . . . well, she didn't want to think about that.

"Sorry, Kyle . . ." Kirsten edged down the sidewalk. "I can't. This is too much. Too deep. Please don't come near me. I never want to see you again!"

She turned and ran, down to Fifth Avenue and around the corner.

Barging into the lobby of her building, she tried to hold back the sobbing. Hector must have thought she was a total soap opera nut. "Sorry, Hector," she said, nearly smashing into the elevator panel as she checked over her shoulder. "I'm okay. Really."

"Miss Kirsten?" Hector replied. "Are you sure?"

Kirsten pressed the button, and the elevator slid open. "*Bueno*," she said as she stepped inside. "Just *bueno*."

The door shut, and Kirsten collapsed onto the upholstered bench opposite the mirror. She looked like shit.

She felt like shit.

About as *bueno* as someone who was in love with a killer could be.

19

"Spike it! *Spike iiiit!*"

The voice of Ms. Gardiner, the Woodley PE teacher, bellowed through the cavernous gymnasium as two teams of volleyball players went at it.

Kirsten felt tired and strung out and about as far from being in the mood for a nice competitive game of volleyball as she could be. Kyle hadn't tried to call her since their fight last night, and she had been reluctant to talk about it with anyone, because anyone in her right mind would tell her to go to the cops right away, to turn him in because her life was at stake. And, of course, Kirsten knew that that was the most reasonable thing to do, but she couldn't. She just couldn't turn Kyle in.

So she told Julie, and only Julie. But all day long kids had been staring at her, whispering behind her back, and Kirsten had the paranoid feeling that somehow the news had gotten out.

On the sidelines, Woodley girls stretched listlessly but picturesquely, waiting to play winners. And Kirsten couldn't help noticing that behind their sad expressions, their devastation over Sam, they were already beginning to come back to normality, to try to establish Life-as-We-Know-It once more, and it bothered her, it cut her to the soul, because it wasn't time yet.

"Do you think Ms. Gardiner is gay?" Leslie asked, strengthening her triceps as she tightened her already perfect ponytail.

"Is Britney a ho?" Carla replied with an overacted yawn.

Sarah attempted a sit-up but fell back to avoid developing an unsightly six-pack. "Why do you ask, Leslie—need a date?"

"Hey, I don't take your sloppy seconds," Leslie shot back.

Kirsten stood up and turned away. "I can't deal with this right now," she muttered to Julie.

"Come on, you need de-stressing. Let's work some sore muscles." Julie took her best friend by the arm and led her to a mat in back of the gym. Because Julie was a class leader and a stealth jock, Ms. Gardiner wasn't likely to bitch and moan.

"So, are you going to tell me what happened between you and Kyle?"

"Julie," Kirsten said, "did you tell anyone about what happened between Kyle and me last night?"

Julie looked slightly offended. "Of *course* not," she said.

"But they all *know* about Kyle and me, don't they? How? How did they find out?"

Julie shrugged. "You know you can't keep a secret at Woodley no matter how hard you try."

Kirsten thought back to last night's argument at the side of her building. The old blowhard in the flannel pj's. "I'll bet Frankie Federman let it out. His dad spotted us."

"Could be, but what's the difference, Kirsten?" Julie asked, touching her forehead to her knee. "Look, the important thing is, you told Kyle to step off. That was great."

"I'm nervous," Kirsten admitted. "I mean, he didn't hurt me yesterday, but what if he's really guilty and I let him get away?" She paused. "I noticed a bunch of missed phone calls on my cell when I was in the courtyard earlier. I didn't recognize the number. Do you think it could be him? What if he comes back for me?"

"For one thing, it isn't going to be easy for him now. Everyone knows who he is. Everyone's looking for him. But frankly, as your friend, that doesn't comfort me. I say call Detective Peterson! Like, now. But if you don't want to do that, if you really think that Kyle *wasn't* feeding you a load of crap . . ."

Julie did a halfhearted yoga stretch while keeping an eye on Ms. Gardiner, who was likely to force volleyball on them if they weren't going through some sort of motions. Kirsten followed her lead.

"But you don't know him, Julie," she said. "If you did, you'd understand how I feel. The Kyle I know is not like that mug shot in the newspaper. He's sensitive and thoughtful and kind and . . . he wears a *Sesame Street* shirt, for God sakes!"

Julie stopped stretching and leaned in close. "I hate to say it, Kirsten, but what you're saying sounds *really* familiar. Like every time you hear the news about some shy, sweet geek who turns out to have killed, like, a million people or something. *'Nope, I had no idea Jeff Dahmer was carrying around a human head in his bowling ball case. He was a great guy, the best player in the league! I can't believe he turned out to be a psychopathic killer who ate people!'"* She paused for a dramatic effect. "Serial killers fool people time after time, Kirsten. How do you think they become *serial?"*

There was no way Kirsten could concentrate on her classes. For the rest of the day she kept thinking about what Julie had said in gym, then what Kyle had told her last night, then back to Julie's advice. Then she started thinking about Brandon and his missing tie, and then Emma and how weird she had been acting lately too. By the end of eighth period she was more confused than ever. To make it worse, she had received two more mystery calls on her cell, which she ignored, but as she pulled her stuff out of her locker, she felt as if the phone were burning a hole in her pocket.

She was tired and cranky. Her math book

was wedged on the top shelf underneath a pile of magazines. She gave a good, hard yank— and everything came crashing to the floor. *"Shit!"* she cried out.

"Gesundheit," Brandon replied from behind her. He was smiling—smarmily.

Kirsten rolled her eyes, ignoring him. She knew that Brandon had heard the rumors about her and Kyle—by now, everybody at Woodley had—and he was probably looking forward to an opportunity to rub her face in it. Kirsten wasn't in the mood. She shoved the magazines in, took her math book, and split.

"What's the hurry?" Brandon said. "Got a date?"

"Screw you, Brandon." Kirsten hurried down the hallway, but Brandon was faster. He ran around her, blocking her way.

He looked awful: hair greasy, chin unshaven, his eyes dilated . . .

"I hear you were at the Party Room last night, but you bounced," he said. "Guess you recovered from Sam's death pretty quick, huh? I hear Emma was there, too, crying on your shoulder." He leaned closer, which gave Kirsten the opportunity to get a whiff of his rank breath. It had to be at least 100 proof. "I know that bitch said something about me. What did she tell you? What?!"

He had this crazed look in his eyes that kind of scared her, but showing fear was not how you handled Brandon Yardley. He was like a dog—once he knew you were afraid of him, he'd hunt you down and rip you to pieces. "Why don't you ask her?" Kirsten said. "And be sure to be just as charming as you are right now. I'm sure she'll open right up. She always does, for you."

"The cops came to my house last night, Kirsten. They asked all these questions," Brandon admitted. *"What did she say?"*

"If they came to your house, then *they* told you what she said, and you already know," Kirsten said. "And frankly, I'm glad they came. It shows that they're still thinking about the case, Brandon, that they realize Sam's killer may not be the obvious suspect."

"What the hell is *that* supposed to mean?" Brandon said, his eyes gaining focus and heat. A crowd was beginning to gather now, but Brandon didn't care. "You're such a bitch, Kirsten. You don't care about anybody else, do you? Just yourself and your goddamn clothes—and all the stupid-ass guys you think you can twist around your finger. That's the way it was with you and Sam, wasn't it? You were laughing at me Friday night. You think you're really hot. Well, okay, you asked for it. *You asked for it!*" His face turned a deep crimson as he reached into his jacket pocket.

What is he pulling out from his jacket? Kirsten backed away slowly, her heart thudding hard in her chest. "Brandon, everybody's watching," she said. "What are you doing?"

"It's your fault, Kirsten," he told her, stepping forward. "You're making me do this. But that's what you wanted, isn't it?" He pulled his hand out quickly—holding a picture. A four-by-five photo.

And Brandon was leaning into her, waving the image in her face. "See . . . that's who you *really* want, isn't it?"

Kirsten struggled to control her frantic heartbeats. She recognized the image right away. Brandon had taken it Friday night at the Party Room. There was Kirsten and Julie. And Sam.

Look at her, look at Sam. . . . She was dancing. They all were. It was the moment after she had flashed Brandon, taunting him, and he was shooting photos continually. She looked irritated, mocking—but *alive,* so incredibly alive—and Kirsten remembered how it felt, how in-your-face Brandon had become that night.

Why is he showing this to me? she thought, turning away. *How did it happen? How did everything go so wrong?* She wanted to go back in time, to jump into the photo and change everything. . . .

"Look at it!" Brandon thrust the picture inches from her face. "Go ahead, look at every face and tell me who you see!"

Kirsten took the photo from Brandon and held it close, her eyes scanning the faces of her friends and the more blurred faces at the edges—Josh Bergen and Frankie Federman, Trevor Royce . . .

But there was another face, staring at the camera but not exactly *in* the crowd. It was a reflection in the mirror over the bar. Peering out from the gawkers, the face happened to have caught the glare from Brandon's flash, and his features were sharp and bright.

Kirsten put her hand to her mouth. She

knew the face. She hadn't seen him there Friday night, hadn't suspected he'd been in the same room, but back then she hadn't known him. And it dawned on her that in all their conversations since, he hadn't told her he was there, in fact he had *lied*—had said he was in the Hamptons!

"Recognize your boyfriend, Kirsten?" Brandon asked. "Recognize Paul Stone?"

20

"He was *there* Friday night, Julie," Kirsten said, leaning over a drink at the Party Room that evening, still reeling from her earlier run-in with Brandon. It was just she and Julie tonight. As much as she loved the rest of her friends, she didn't need a crowd right now. She needed one sympathetic ear and mind, to help her sort things out. "Kyle was in the Party Room," Kirsten went on. "I saw his face in Brandon's picture, reflected in the mirror. But last night Kyle told me—right to my face—that he was in the Hamptons on Friday. He *lied* to me. And the worst part was, he wanted me to give an alibi. He wanted me to cover for *his* lie!"

Julie put a hand gently on Kirsten's shoulder. "This must be so hard, Kirsten. You really fell for him, huh?"

"I'm just so confused, Jules. I mean, Kyle

was so convincing. He showed me his Talcott tie. He still has it. And Brandon is missing his. And with all Brandon's rage and violent behavior . . . I just thought maybe . . ."

"Come on." Julie put a hand on Kirsten's shoulder. "You do know Kyle could have gotten another tie anywhere . . . right?"

Kirsten nodded and took a slow sip of her drink. She knew that she was grasping at straws, but she couldn't help it. What was wrong with her? Why was it so hard for her to fully commit to the idea that Kyle was Sam's killer?

"I—I don't know, Julie . . . I just have this . . . *feeling*," Kirsten said. "It's hard to explain. I know Kyle lied, and I know it looks really bad . . . but against all reason, something inside my gut is telling me that he didn't do it."

"But Kirsten, his face was in the picture," Julie said. "He was there. He lied. Why else would he have lied if he wasn't trying to cover something up?"

Kirsten shook her head and stared into her drink. "Last night, I tried to put myself in his shoes . . . tried to imagine I'd been accused of something I didn't do, that I'd been put in jail and then released. I tried to picture life with this cloud over my head, and then finally making up my mind to come back to the scene of the crime to prove my innocence—only to have another horrible murder happen, *which is exactly like the one I'd been accused of before.*" She glanced at Julie. "And I asked myself, would I tell the truth if I knew people would place me near the scene of a crime that I didn't do, which matched the *other* one I didn't do—would I be tempted to lie?"

Julie listened silently, mixing her drink.

"All we know is, Kyle was *there,*" Kirsten went on. "Just like you and I were there. We don't know that he left with Sam. It hasn't been released that Friday was the night Sam died. It could have been Saturday or Sunday or even Monday. The picture may not mean anything. There are still so many other questions, Julie. Like, what did Brandon do after I saw him that night? And that red-haired guy—no one's heard from him at all."

"I guess he should have contacted the police when he heard the reports," Julie said quietly.

"Yes," Kirsten said, "if he was innocent."

"He might have been able to help," Julie admitted. "He was the last person to see Sam alive."

"We're not even sure of *that* . . . ," Kirsten replied, taking a final sip and emptying her glass.

Scott walked over with a concerned expression. "How's it going? You guys look pretty serious over here. Can I get you anything?"

"You're the best, Scott." Julie looked at her watch. "I've got to go, though. My parents don't want me to stay out so late anymore. If we leave now, we can walk home. It's beautiful out."

Going outside sounded great to Kirsten. She was feeling a little claustrophobic. "Thanks, Scott. See you soon."

"Feel better, guys," he said.

Kirsten and Julie walked out of the bar and into the clear night. Kirsten pulled her cute little cashmere blazer closed against the dry chill in the air, which hinted that winter was just around the corner. Walking up Second Avenue, she could smell distant burning fireplaces, and then it occurred to her why Julie had suggested the walk. Partly for the fresh air and weather, but also for the memories.

On every street was some story, sweet or funny or painful, that involved Sam. In a way, recalling those stories felt like a good way of saying good-bye.

"Sam loved this farmers' market," Kirsten said, gesturing to a corner stand covered for the night by a corrugated-steel gate. "She said it was because of the fresh fruit, but really it was because they always gave her free candy. The owner was in love with her."

"They all were," Julie said with a laugh.

The girls passed bar after bar, each with its own memory, until they got to Eighty-third Street, where they would turn to go home. There, on the corner, was a brand-new club called Janus.

"Oh God, you know what Sam would have said about this," Kirsten said.

Julie howled. "Sure: 'What happens if the "J" light blows?'"

"Then it becomes a different kind of bar," Kirsten remarked, checking out the entryway.

The décor was totally from the 1980s, with lots of brushed steel and black-and-white surrounding the door. Kirsten gazed through the big plate-glass window to the left of it. Inside, people were dancing, but there was a small crowd of Dalton and Spence preparatory kids surrounding a high table, drinking beers and eating nachos. Then she saw a shock of red hair only briefly, moving behind the window crowd.

Kirsten stopped. It was impossible to tell for sure, but the cut seemed similar, and the height was about right. "Did you see that?" she asked. "The red hair?"

Julie raised an eyebrow. "Kirsten, a lot of people have red hair. Let's go. It's getting late."

No. Kirsten couldn't leave without checking. She wouldn't have been able to stop wondering. "Let me just take a look, okay? Just wait here a second. If it's him, I'll come tell you. We can call Peterson."

Julie looked at her watch. "Make it quick, okay?"

Kirsten entered the club and made her way to the bar. The techno-pop house music irritated her, echoing harshly off the polished black floor and metal ceiling. She slithered among the dancers, looking for the red hair but not seeing it.

Oh, well, she thought. *At least I tried.* She turned to head back, and noticed that there was another room off to her left. She peeked into the room and breathed in a thick cloud of marijuana smoke. She should have figured. When the cloud lifted she noticed a stoned-looking Goth girl slouched on a fuzzy black chair, holding her hand underneath a low white table.

On the other side of the table was a man with red hair, pulled back into a ponytail.

Kirsten moved closer as he told a joke that failed to amuse his partner.

He smiled, and it was the smile that did it. The same smile she'd seen at the Party Room.

The same smile he'd given Sam, before leaving with her for the last time.

Purely by accident, Kirsten had found Sam's mysterious red-haired man.

21

"Hello?" Kirsten said.

"Excuse me?"

The guy stopped talking to the Goth girl and stared at her through bloodshot eyes.

Yes. It was him. Definitely. The choice of partner was an interesting twist—about as different from Sam as could possibly be—but the profile, the ruddy skin, the strong features and jaw were dead on.

He nodded at Kirsten. "What's up?" he said through a smirk.

"Can I talk to you for a minute? About my friend, Samantha Byrne?"

The guy squinted. "What? Who?" he said.

"Last Friday night . . . the Party Room? Long blond hair? Really beautiful? You left with her." Kirsten shrugged at the guy's companion, who was chewing gum with her mouth open. "Sorry, but he did."

"I don't know what you're talking about," the guy drawled.

"Sam Byrne—you know, the girl in the news, the one who was . . ."

They were both looking at her blankly, as if neither of them had watched TV or picked up a newspaper all week. She hated having to spell it out, to say the words. "She was killed. In Central Park. They haven't found the murderer, but you were with her the last time she was seen in public, so I thought you might know something."

"Do you have . . . a picture?" the guy asked, his voice a little slow and drawn too, and Kirsten realized he was probably stoned out of his mind, and it would take a lot to get him to focus.

Kirsten pulled around her bag and began rummaging through it for a photo. "Sure. Let me take a look. . . ."

The guy leaned forward, rising from his seat, peering into Kirsten's bag. Kirsten glanced at him for a second. He was tall, about six one, and seemed a little shaky. She kept searching through her purse and finally found her wallet. "Here," she said, pulling out a recent shot of the two of them mugging for the camera on Woodley Hill. God, she missed Sam.

But when she looked up, he was gone, darting among the dancers toward the bar.

Kirsten took off. She ran after him, getting to the bar as he disappeared behind it, and followed him into a narrow hallway that led past the kitchen and the bathrooms. At the end of the hall was a metal door with a sign that said, FIRE EXIT—DO NOT OPEN, ALARM WILL SOUND.

Kirsten pushed it without any alarm sounding and emerged into a dark alley. To the left, the alley ended in a brick wall. To the right was a line of trash cans, leading to East Eighty-third Street. The guy was past the cans already, his sneakers thumping the concrete, and he turned left, up Eighty-third toward Third Avenue.

Kirsten could hear the clamor of clubgoers around the corner, on Second Avenue. Julie would be there, waiting, but there was no time to get her.

She raced to the street and looked to the left, up the block. It inclined upward to Third. On the uptown side, the air-conditioning unit to some institutional building belched hot air onto the sidewalk. The downtown side, just

past a construction site, was a wall of tene-
ments and old brownstones.

But the sidewalks on both sides were empty.

This guy was fast, incredibly fast. The distance to Third Avenue was huge, a long
cross-town New York City block. It seemed
impossible to get so far so fast. Especially for
someone stoned.

Kirsten was racing now, running up the
block without thinking, her feet barely touching the pavement, her eyes burning, her mind
struggling with the possibility that this guy—
a total stranger, a stoner no one had seen
before, who had happened into the Party
Room one night, maybe for the first time—
might have singled out Sam.

As she reached the end of the construction
site she slipped on some concrete dust, against
a stack of cinderblocks. In the shadow of the
blocks, a shape moved. Kirsten was off-
balance, unable to react fast enough.

As she struggled to right herself, it sprang
toward her.

Screaming, Kirsten jumped aside. The red-
haired guy sped past her, out to the sidewalk,
and began to run.

He was clumsy, flat-footed. Kirsten regained her balance and took chase. He ran like someone who had been smoking dope, and despite the fact that Ms. Gardiner, the gym teacher, had nearly flunked Kirsten in track and field, she was gaining on him.

She could hear his labored breathing as they both approached Third Avenue, and she jumped, arms extended, closing them around his legs as she fell to the sidewalk.

He stumbled down with her, and they rolled to the right, landing against the wheels of a gray Toyota parked smack against the curb—and she held him, tightly. She had run him down. After days of being beaten about emotionally by Brandon and Kyle and Emma, she was on top this time.

"What . . . what the . . . ?" he stammered.

Kirsten scrambled forward, sitting on his chest. "What happened that night?" she demanded. "Where did you go with Sam?"

"Out, that's all," he said.

"What's your name?" Kirsten demanded.

"What's it to you?"

"You went to Talcott, didn't you? Talcott Prep. You had the tie!"

"Freeport High School. A long time ago." He fixed an icy stare on her, and a creepy chill ran down Kirsten's back. "You'd better get off of me before I get angry," he said. "You don't want to get me angry."

"Kirsten?" Julie's voice called from behind her. "KIRSTE-E-E-ENNNNN!"

Kirsten turned. "Over here!" she cried, waving a hand.

The red-haired guy pushed. Kirsten lost her balance and fell back. He slipped away, jumping to his feet, and ran.

Kirsten took chase again, but he was in the street now, waving down a taxi, which had to swerve to avoid him.

As Kirsten squeezed between parked cars and into the street, he was climbing inside the back of the cab. She grabbed the handle of the door as it shut, and the taxi peeled around the corner, leaving her behind.

"Oh my God," Julie said, running up to her, out of breath. "Kirsten, are you okay? What happened? How did you get here? What did he do to you?"

"Nothing," Kirsten said. "I pinned *him*."

"You did? How? *Why?*"

Kirsten caught her breath. She'd had him. She'd almost gotten his story. *Almost!* "He ran when I asked him about Sam. He was wasted, Julie. That was the only reason I could get him. I got the feeling he gets wasted a lot. He admitted going somewhere with Sam, but wouldn't tell me where. He said he didn't go to Talcott, and knows nothing about a tie."

"Thank God you're okay, Kirsten," Julie said, taking out her cell phone. "But you shouldn't have done this alone. I'm calling the police."

Brushing off the sidewalk gravel from her knees, Kirsten wondered what good she'd done. She hadn't gotten the red-haired guy's name. She wasn't any closer to knowing who Sam's killer was. And she made someone who may have killed Sam pissed off at *her.* Nothing about tonight made Kirsten feel better.

As Julie tapped out the number for Peterson—a number they all knew by heart— Kirsten slung an arm around her friend's shoulders, and they both started home.

She kept a wary eye on her surroundings, though, because she had the oddest feeling. A feeling that she was being watched . . .

22

I never imagined I'd bring HER into this, but this one has a big mouth, doesn't she. I don't like all the talking.

"NO TALKING!" I tell her.

I have to stop it, or they're all going to suspect. It may be too late. They may ALL think I'm involved, and how's that for trying to stay under the radar, trying to be in CONTROL and failing.

Aw, look. She's starting to cry. So sensitive. So sweet.

"You know you brought it on yourself," I say nicely, but I don't have much patience for her sniveling.

"NO SNIVELING!" I say.

It's late. I'm tired. Well, of course. I didn't go out and get her until two A.M. And with that, I was lucky. What a surprise to find her.

Now, where did I put those special pills?

It was hard to get so many of them. Ah. Here . . .

Ten little pills . . . twenty little pills . . . cute ones, grind 'em up good, put 'em in the milkshake. WHIIIRRRR goes the blender, smells like fruit smoothie, tastes like fruit smoothie. These will fit nicely into that BIG MOUTH!

She's shaking now. Good. Maybe she'll think next time. NEXT TIME. Ha-ha.

Up goes the hankie, off the mouth. So easy. Well, that's what happens when you flirt with them and get them drunk.

No need for nitrous oxide tonight. She can hear my voice. I don't care, she's not going anywhere after this.

"Open up," I tell her. "It's to give you strength, come on, you have an empty stomach . . . remember—scream and you get NO FOOD. Here. That's it, open wide. . . . You'll need it. It will help with the BIG headache you're going to have."

Ha-ha. I'm so funny today. It won't help her headache. Nothing can help. But THAT'S WHAT YOU GET WHEN YOU HAVE A BIG MOUTH AND MAKE PEOPLE GO SNOOPING INTO MY BUSINESS!

Come on, hold still. There. There it goes. Down the hatch.

The hard part is over.

Oh. Yes. Almost forgot . . .
Now where oh where did I put that tie?
Shit. Shit shit shit. I used it.
Well, then, I'll need something else, won't I. . . .

Part Three

23

"I looked at the mug shots for hours, but I didn't see anyone who looked like Red," Kirsten told Julie over the phone. It was almost noon, and she'd just returned home from the police station. "They obviously don't have a thing on this guy. Last night they called Janus and the owner said no one had ever heard of him. They asked about the girl who was with him, too, but she was long gone. Peterson says he went around to every bar in the neighborhood, from Ninety-sixth to Seventy-second, but had no luck. It's like this guy doesn't exist, Julie. Like he's a phantom."

Kirsten shifted down the length of her mattress, propping her feet on one of the posts of her four-poster bed. She wanted to forget this morning's interview. It had been the worst way to begin a weekend. Peterson hadn't taken her into a private room this time. She had to talk about Sam's death and possible murderer right in the main part of the station house, with cops walking in and out, walkie-talkies blaring—Kirsten had never seen so many Dunkin' Donuts take-out bags in her life. "Well, I did the best I could. It was weird. Kyle's picture—the old Paul Stone shot from the *Post*—is all over the walls."

"You told Peterson about Kyle, too, right?" Julie asked. "About what happened the other night?"

Kirsten cringed. She knew Julie was going to ask this. And Kirsten had come close to telling Peterson, but somehow she just couldn't. She had a bad feeling. The news reports were full of attacks on the police, saying they botched the arrest of Paul Stone two years ago by destroying evidence and not following procedure and all that. Kirsten knew the cops wanted Kyle badly, and maybe it was for all the right reasons or maybe they wanted to hurry up and get him in jail so that all the negative press would go away. Somehow she couldn't be the one to deliver him to them. . . . "No. I didn't tell him."

"You *didn't?* Kirsten, what's the matter with you? You still think he won't be treated fairly? *That's not for you to decide!*"

"I know. I know, Julie. It may be the stupidest thing I ever didn't do—" Kirsten was interrupted by the beep of an incoming call. "Sorry. Talk later, okay? Gotta go. . . ." She pressed the Call button. "Hello?"

For a second, no one answered. And then a soft male voice said, "Kirsten, it's me. Kyle."

Kirsten sat up. "Kyle?"

"It's so good to hear your voice. Listen, I can't talk long. I have to see you. Right away—"

Kirsten was shaking. She didn't know why. No, she *did* know why. It was relief and happiness and fear and resentment and anger and mistrust, all of them mixed together in her mind, held inside and making her want to burst. "You . . . you lied to me, Kyle. You weren't in the Hamptons Friday night. You were at the Party Room, weren't you?"

There was a long pause. "Yeah, I was. I was hoping you wouldn't find out before I had the chance to tell you. That was one of the things I was calling about."

She wanted to believe him. She was so eager to believe that he was trying to be honest, that at least he had *planned* to come clean, that she had to take a deep breath, slow herself down, and force her mind into some rational, obvious, right-brain thinking: *She* had mentioned the lie, not him. Maybe he *hadn't* been calling to admit he'd been at the Party Room. Maybe that was another lie. "Kyle, how can you expect me to trust you? How can I know what's the truth and what isn't?"

"I've been thinking a lot about those things—about lies—ever since we . . . talked. And I realize I can't do it anymore. I can't keep it up. You're right, the more I try to run from this, the worse it gets. I can't live a life built on lies. I know that. I'm going to the police tonight, Kirsten. I'm going to tell them the truth—all of it, even if I know they won't believe me. I wanted to clear my name, but now, with Sam's murder, I don't think it's possible. I wish I could find out who did it, but I can't keep going on like this. I can't keep running."

"I found the red-haired guy, Kyle," Kirsten said. "The one who left the Party Room with

Sam. I saw him at a club last night. He's creepy, Kyle."

"*Really?*" Kyle sounded hopeful. "Did the police pick him up? Who is he?"

"I don't know," Kirsten said. "He got away from me. And the police don't have any leads on him yet."

"Well, it's a start," Kyle said slowly. "It means there may be a chance for me after I turn myself in."

He was still going to go to the cops. He wasn't going to back out. It was a good decision, a truthful one. "Good luck, Kyle," she said.

She heard Kyle sigh. "Which means, Kirsten, I may not see you for a long time. Forever, maybe. I'd like to see you now. Is that all right? Will you meet me?"

His voice was soft and vulnerable, and she went down the mental checklist of all the things that made her mistrust him—there had been so many lies. But maybe he really had figured it out: that, in the end, the truth was all you had. He hadn't proven himself yet, but she was willing to give him the benefit of the doubt. For now. "Okay, Kyle," she said. "But I'm nervous."

"I understand," Kyle replied. "We'll meet in a public place. Before dark. Like, in front of the Met."

"Too close to home," Kirsten said. "Let's do it by the Alice in Wonderland statue in the park, near Seventy-second Street." There would be little kids around, nannies with big mouths and cell phones—just in case. She looked at her watch. "Fifteen minutes. See you there."

Fourteen minutes later, Kirsten was winding her way down the footpath toward the statue. Clouds were gathering overhead, but the park was packed with people. Through the trees she saw the masts of radio-controlled miniature sailboats gliding across the pond. The official Parks Department name for it was Conservatory Water, but it was really the Stuart Little pond, of course. When she was a kid she had spent hours looking for him— Stuart—on all the little sailboats. Her first unrequited love. A boy born as a mouse. How simple life was back then, before she'd discovered what she knew now: that boys couldn't be mice at all, but they could grow up to be rats.

"Would you like to join me for tea? Pull up a mushroom." Kyle was sitting on the tiny bronze mushroom seat of the Alice statue, leaning over the bronze mushroom table, across from the Mad Hatter. He was dressed in a black, flowing cotton shirt that accentuated his shoulders, and his soft hair picked up the light of the setting sun.

She was toast.

Although a hundred loud voices in her head still said, *Get out while you can,* she listened to the rising chorus of, *Go for it.* She went to him, slowly at first, and he stood. "I guess you must be pretty scared of me," he said softly.

And he was right, a part of her was scared, but when she looked at his uncertain, questioning smile, the notion of being *scared of him* evaporated from her mind, and she suddenly found herself in his arms, holding him and not wanting to doubt or think at all.

This was why she had wanted to see him in public, she realized. Not because she was afraid of him. Because she was afraid of *herself.* Because she knew she'd want exactly what she wanted right now. Something so private that their meeting had to be out in the open for her own good.

"I missed you," Kyle said.

"Kyle," Kirsten said, "I need a promise from you. That as long as we're here, it's all truth between you and me."

Kyle nodded.

"I want to say I've missed you. I have and I haven't. If you disappeared right now, my life would be so much easier. Can you understand that?" He looked wounded, and she snuggled her head in his shoulder. "But we're supposed to tell the truth, and the truth is, I *don't* want you to go. And against my better judgment, and my friend's advice, I want to give you a chance. But we have to take this slow, Kyle. Very slow."

A few yards away, a face-lifted mom grinned at them. "We were like that once," she said to her buttoned-down-and-balding husband, who looked as if his memory chip suddenly needed replacement.

"Um, maybe we should get out of here," Kyle said, glancing around.

Kirsten laughed. "Okay. I guess we're setting a bad example for the kids."

She took Kyle's arm, and they wound their way uphill, farther into the park, away from Fifth Avenue and the pond. They took the tunnel under the car road and made a right around the Boathouse, continuing upward on a steep path that led into the heavily wooded part of the park. To their left, on a patch of dirt just off a footpath, Kirsten spotted a huge leathery snapping turtle sitting on her eggs. A light drizzle, which began as they walked up the hill, became a steady rain when they reached the top. Looking down the hill, Kirsten could see people rushing into the Boathouse and toward the park exits. She heard the phone ring in her pocket but ignored it.

Just up the path was a landscape construction site. An unmanned backhoe was parked next to a corrugated construction shed. As the rain pounded their heads, Kyle took Kirsten's hand. "Come on!" he cried.

He pulled her around to the front of the shed. A thick padlock hung uselessly from the broken hasp of the door, so he pulled it open. Inside was a collection of rakes, shovels, rolled-up fencing, metal posts, buckets, and thick rolls of bright yellow CAUTION tape.

Not exactly the Plaza, but dry.

The rain pelted the metal rooftop, sounding like kettledrums, and Kirsten thought she heard her phone again, but Kyle was now offering her a seat next to his, on two overturned buckets.

They sat, arms around each other, listening to the rain. And after a while, Kirsten pulled out her phone. 2 NEW MESSAGES.

"Sorry, Julie's been trying to reach me," she said, calling her voice mail. She held the phone tight to her ear and listened to the recorded message:

"Kirsten . . . Kirsten, oh my God, where are you? Why can't you be there?"

"What's up?" Kyle asked.

"Shhh . . ." Kirsten had to put her finger in her outside ear to block the sound of the rain.

"Did you hear the news?" Julie was crying hysterically. *"Oh, this is so horrible!"*

Kirsten stiffened. Julie was never this out of control—not even at Sam's funeral.

"It's Emma . . . she's dead, Kirsten. They found her. Her head was beaten in, and she was tied up just like Sam was! But the killer didn't use

a tie—he used T-shirt. With, like, Grover on it. Is that sick or what?"

It was sick. Really sick. Kirsten wanted to scream and cry out, but she didn't. Instead, she glanced at Kyle. He had worn a Grover shirt the night she'd been at the dorm. He'd worn it all the way down 112th Street.

Kirsten pulled the phone away from her ear, putting her other hand over the earpiece to keep Kyle from hearing the voice.

As she hit the stop button, he was smiling at her curiously. "Everything okay?"

"Fine," she said, and she worked hard not to show her growing, numbing panic. She stood up and began to back away, as far away from Kyle as she could, toward the wall of the shed.

"Kirsten?" Kyle said. "You look upset. Are you sure everything's all right?"

Tied with a Grover T-shirt . . . she thought, *a Grover T-shirt!*

"Kirsten, what's wrong?" Kyle asked. "Did something happen to Julie?"

He'd promised to tell the truth and had made her promise too. But how could she tell him the truth about what she'd heard? That

Emma had died, strangled by his shirt? Because it *was* his shirt. At some point, you had to stop believing in coincidences. She'd allowed him to fool her about the Talcott tie— but what could he possibly say about a *Grover T-shirt?*

What did the truth mean to Paul Stone?

She'd been a fool. He'd tricked her totally. The red-haired stoner hadn't killed Sam. Neither had Brandon or Emma—Kyle had, *Paul* had.

"Kirsten, talk to me." He rose from the seat, stepped closer to her, and now, even the *sight* of the door was obliterated, and Kirsten realized that she had let herself be led into a shed in the middle of nowhere, into what must have been the only *isolated public spot* in New York City. He was six foot one and strong, and he was between her and the door. She wouldn't stand a chance.

"Well, um, actually, Julie's having some . . . homework problems," Kirsten said, hating the lameness in her own voice. "S-so I should probably go help her out. . . ." She tried to sidestep around him, but the shed was narrow and its walls were crammed with tools and boxes, jamming them both into a kind of narrow corridor, and the *only* way she could get by him would be somehow to squeeze past, which at the moment seemed about impossible.

"The rain will let up in a little while," Kyle said. "Can't you wait a couple of minutes?"

She was instinctively walking toward the door, toward him, which seemed a stupid thing to do to a killer, but he was backing away. Closer to the door. And she realized maybe as long as he kept backing up, this would work. When he was close enough, she could leap by him.

Kyle tilted his head with concern. "You're shaking, Kirsten."

"I—I am?" Kirsten said.

"The truth . . . remember? We have to be honest with each other."

"I know," Kirsten said. "Okay."

He was now a few feet away from the exit. "Julie told you something, didn't she? Something you don't want me to hear. What is it, Kirsten? Can't you tell me?"

Kirsten lunged away, but Kyle was between her and the door. Her foot slipped on the rain-slicked floor and she fell, crashing into a stack of flowerpots. Her cell phone flew out of her hand, and Kyle picked it up.

"It's about me, isn't it?" Kyle asked, staring at the screen. "I need to tell you the truth. Did she say something about me?"

"No," Kirsten said. "I just—I have to go."

Kyle's eyes had lost their strength and sharpness. He was scared, Kirsten could tell— but not as scared as she was. As he began punching in numbers, Kirsten realized he was *replaying her voice mail,* putting her phone to his ear and listening to Julie's voice.

"No!" Kirsten sprang upward and tried to take back the phone, but he held her away, and his face, as he listened, slowly grew red. "Oh, my God . . . *ohhhhhh, no . . . no, no, nooooo!"*

He let the phone drop and turned around as if lost, as if trying to find his bearings. "So you think . . . because of that . . ."

"Just give me the phone, Kyle," Kirsten said, "and step away. Please. Let me go."

Suddenly, with an odd, strangled-sounding cry, he reared his arm back and punched the wall of the shed, and Kirsten cringed.

Kyle's face lost its color. "I'm dead!" He yelled. "They're going to send me to jail for the rest of my life! I'm dead!" He smashed his fist against the opposite wall.

While he wasn't looking, while there was an inch of space, Kirsten scooped up her phone and made a break for it, pushing Kyle aside and barreling into the door, shoulder first.

It swung open, letting in the cool rain. Her feet slipped on the debris, and she stumbled, reaching out with her arms to steady herself.

Kyle held her back, taking her by the arm. "Where are you going? Can't you see? *This* is what happens when you try to tell the truth. Someone has to be out to get me. Somebody wants to ruin my life! How can I tell the truth, Kirsten? I was so stupid to think it would work!"

"*Let me go!*" she shouted.

Kyle pulled her back and yanked the door shut. "You can't go," he said. "I need you. They found the shirt. The damn *Grover shirt*, Kirsten. They'll lock me up forever. Oh God, you have to back me up. You have to tell them you were with me last night. That I was nowhere near Emma."

227

"I *wasn't* with you last night. *I won't lie!*" Somehow, Kirsten had found the courage to say it.

"You have to see what's going on. It won't work if you don't stick with me—just this time. Just so I can get away. I need you, Kirsten. Will you do it? Will you?"

This time, she didn't feel it. She didn't feel the tug of his personality, the instinct that made her want to give in, to trust him. All she felt now was another instinct, the will to survive against a killer, against someone who was deluded or evil or both, and she made a sudden desperate break for the door again.

Kyle slammed it shut. The roar of the wind became muffled.

Kyle took her by the shoulders and pulled her deeper into the shed. In the closeness of the space, his perspiration was steaming from his shoulders, dissipating into the cool air. "You will say yes, Kirsten," he said, "if you want to leave this place."

24

"Yes."

Kirsten heard herself speak, but it didn't feel like a word; rather, a reflex from some other part of her body, like the sudden jerk of a hand away from an electric shock.

"What did you say?" Kyle asked.

"I said, yes," she repeated, consciously now. "I'll lie for you."

Kyle loosened his grip, but not by much. He was still scared, his eyes wild. "We can't think of it as a lie. It's just buying time until we can build a case—because that's what we have to do, Kirsten. The cops won't, even though it's their job. We have to come to the table with another story. Tell me more about the red-haired guy. Did he jump you? Did he pull a knife or anything?"

"No, he just ran away. *I* jumped on *him*, but he escaped when I turned to signal Julie."

Kyle nailed her with his eyes. "He threatened you. He dragged you into an alley and said he was going to kill you. He had a backpack and he started to pull something out of it—you couldn't tell what it was, but it looked like a long, rolled-up piece of clothing—when all of a sudden, Julie called you. She came running up the street with a bunch of other kids, and he realized he was outnumbered, so he ran."

"Okay." Kirsten swallowed her disgust.

"Give him words. He said, 'You saw me that night at the Party Room. You got a good look at my face. So you're next.' Something like that."

Kirsten nodded, silently, but Kyle seemed to grow more tense and irritated.

"The cops will believe you, Kirsten. They'll give you the benefit of the doubt. And we'll be able to find the real killer on our own. I know we will."

All Kirsten could do was stare at him, thinking over and over, *He's insane . . . completely insane. . . .*

Kyle pulled her farther into the shed, gesturing for her to sit on an overturned bucket, and she did, leaning forward, keeping the weight on her feet in case she had the chance somehow to bolt.

"You have to understand what the last two years have been like." Kyle was speaking so fast now, he nearly tripped over his words. "It wasn't only me. After I was released, my parents were getting death threats over the phone. They had to quit their jobs and move. You wouldn't believe what they had to pay Randall Luis Gringer to take my case. It nearly bankrupted them. We won, but what good did it do? The media angle was: The cops blew it, and the court let off a killer on a technicality. So not only did everyone assume I was guilty, the cops were embarrassed. We showed them up, Kirsten. And now they're pissed. They want revenge and they're just waiting for me to stumble, and *the real killer knows it*. He's using me to get away with murder!"

The idea that Kyle had been represented by Randall Luis Gringer—a.k.a. Gold-Plated Gringer, Counsel to the Stars, Lawyer of the Loophole, with his custom-designed suits and personal fleet of private jets—didn't impress Kirsten, because Gringer could get anyone off.

But the intensity of Kyle's emotion struck her like a cold slap, because he didn't realize how crazy he sounded. He thought he sounded logical, like a rational person hurt by circumstances beyond his control, and it dawned on Kirsten that he *believed* he was innocent, that he'd created this whole story to hide behind, to deny the things he'd done—that, to him, they weren't lies because *he really thought they were true.*

She knew she had to appeal to that logic. "Kyle, a minute ago you said you were going to go to the police to tell them the whole story, the truth—"

"A minute ago I didn't know they'd find a Grover shirt on Emma's body!" Kyle said. "Here's the truth, Kirsten: *I didn't do it.* It's not lying if it's to protect the truth. Is it?"

He was standing firm, legs apart, his right foot almost touching the battered scoop of a sturdy shovel, its handle resting upright against the wall. It was angled forward from Kyle, within reach of Kirsten.

She leaned forward slightly.

"The point is," Kyle said, "someone killed Sam, and since it wasn't me, it had to be the red-haired guy. We all saw him leave the Party Room with Sam. You said he was a creep. He's the only one who could have done this. So how can we let him get away with it? We tell them he attacked you, and afterward you called me, and we were together all night, including the time that Emma was killed. It's not all about truth, Kirsten. It's about justice. It's about keeping this guy from doing anything bad ever again."

Outside, the wind sent a sudden blast, sending the fallen branch of a tree against the side of the shed with a sharp *smack.*

Kyle jumped, looking toward the noise.

And Kirsten found herself leaping up, grabbing, her fingers closing around the shaft of the shovel handle.

"What the—," Kyle said.

But he didn't have time to finish, because Kirsten was swinging, twisting from the hips, throwing her weight into the sweep of the shovel blade through the air until it made contact with Kyle's lower back.

He lurched forward with a startled grunt and fell to his knees, then forward onto his chest. "Kirst—"

Kirsten dropped the shovel and ran for the door. She tripped over cans, nearly invisible in the stingy light of the shed, and grabbed the door handle.

It was stuck. Kyle had pulled it too hard and had jammed it.

"Ohhhhh . . . ," came Kyle's voice.

She glanced behind her. His shoulder blades were rising. He was pushing himself up. Kirsten banged on the handle, pounded on the door with her shoulders and hips. "Help! Help me! Somebody! Help!"

Behind her, she heard Kyle stumbling to his feet. And before she knew it, Kyle's fingers were around her collar and he was pulling hard, choking her, making her lose her footing as he dragged her into the shed.

He released her, and she fell against a machine, a spreader of some kind, tucked into the farthest corner from the door. She looked around for something, anything that she could use to defend herself.

Kyle was stepping toward her now, his eyes wide with a mix of emotions that Kirsten couldn't quite read, and his mouth was moving as if he was trying to say something.

"Let me go, Kyle," she said. "You don't want to do this. You know that, right?"

"You're going to betray me . . . ," he replied, his voice barely more than a whisper.

Kirsten grabbed on to a nearby rake and held it in front of her. "I don't want to hurt you, Kyle. But I will. I'll use this unless you push that door open."

He wasn't answering and he wasn't afraid; instead, he calmly reached over to the wall behind him, where a spool of yellow tape hung on a hook. It was the plastic tape used to cordon off construction sites, and he was unwinding a length of it, twisting it as he did until he had at least thirty feet, then ripping it from the spool and doubling and tripling it.

He was doing it so matter-of-factly, as if making a tourniquet or repairing a piece of equipment. "This won't hurt," he said.

Kirsten swung the rake, hard. Kyle jumped back, calmly timing her swing. And as her momentum pulled her around, he lunged, grabbing her arms and quickly wrapping, wrapping the tape around her wrists.

"*STOP!*" Kirsten shrieked. "*POLICE! POLIIIIICE!*"

The sound was muffled. Pathetic. With the rain pounding the roof, she had trouble even hearing herself, and Kyle was working fast, pushing her down onto an old wooden seat, threading the tape around her thumbs and binding her fingers together. "Does this hurt?" he said. "I don't want it to hurt."

"YES, IT HURTS!"

It hurt like crazy, but it hurt even more knowing he was going to kill her, and she looked around frantically because now everything around her, every object, was a potential weapon she could use to kill him first, if she could get up somehow, if she could break through the plastic tape . . .

"I don't want to do anything to cause you pain, Kirsten," he said, making a knot. "I just needed to buy time. I thought you understood that. But you were fooling me, pretending to go along. You lied. That's the ironic thing, Kirsten. We were talking about justice and truth, and you *lied!*"

At that last word he gritted his teeth, pulling the knot tight. "Just one more step," he said, and he grabbed the spool and unrolled the tape around her legs, binding her to the seat. "This will be so much easier for you if you don't struggle."

"YOU CAN'T GET AWAY WITH THIS, KYLE! HELLLP!" She tried to kick him, but he was too strong, and when her legs were secure he stood and wrapped the tape around her upper arms. His shoulder was against her chest now, and she could feel his breath and see the raindrops on his hair, matting it into brown clumps.

His left ear was inches from her mouth.

She thrust her head forward, her teeth clamping around the ear, and she bit. Hard.

Kyle shrieked and reeled backward. "God *damn* it! *Shit!* You're an animal! You're a fuck-ing animal!"

She yanked on the tape, but she was stuck. He'd done his work well. She was bound to the chair, neck to ankle. She lurched up and down, the chair banging noisily on the floor.

Kyle stepped forward. His ear was bleeding, dripping onto the floor, pooling with the rainwater, but Kirsten wasn't watching him. She was only moving, pulling, jerking, working the tape, *yes*, it was coming loose and she strained even harder. . . .

"You're making me do this, Kirsten," he said, standing over her now, bent at the waist, keeping his upper body safely distant from her. "I didn't want to. I never would have dreamed of it. But you were going to betray me. . . ."

Then Kyle stretched a length of tape between his hands and looped it around Kirsten's neck. . . .

25

"**No!**" she cried out, feeling the rough edge of the tape touch the back of her neck. "NO-O-O-O! *Don't kill me, too!* You said you loved me, Kyle. How can you do this to someone you love?"

Kyle paused, his hands on either side of her, the tape pressing against her neck. "Kill you, too? My God, you really *believe* them, don't you?" He knelt, looking into her eyes.

"No, I don't," Kirsten said, lying through her teeth. This was all about survival now. "I just got scared, that's all. I'll help you. I'll do whatever you want."

Kyle shook his head. "I can't trust you anymore. Don't you see what just happened? We had it all planned out. It would have worked. Don't you see how bad it is to screw things up with a lie? Sorry, Kirsten."

His hands drew together, bringing the tape

around front. And Kirsten did the only thing she could think of doing.

She spat in his face.

Kyle flinched, and Kirsten leaned into him, tilting forward on the chair's legs. She went over, taking him with her, making him fall into the blade of a backhoe. He yowled in pain and collapsed, moaning.

On her side, Kirsten wriggled her legs until she was able to work the tape over the bottoms of the chair legs. She pulled her legs free, the tape going slack, and was able to stand. As she yanked her body from side to side, the chair swung until it fell away.

Legs free, hands free, she ran for the door.

Behind her she could hear Kyle struggling to his feet. This time she propped her foot against the wall to the left of the knob as she pulled. The added leverage worked, the door flew open, and she ran.

The rain had let up somewhat, but the sun had set, and through the trees she saw red tail lights turning away from the small field where she was. "HELLLP!" she screamed, running.

It was a police car, Central Park precinct. Even before she reached it, two cops had jumped out and were rushing toward her. *"There's a murderer in the shed—over there!"* she screamed, pointing.

The door to the shed was wide open.

The younger of the two officers seemed frightened. "Is he armed?" he asked.

"No," Kirsten said.

The older partner, gray-haired and over-weight, stepped forward. "Let's find him." They were on a blacktop path, and he stepped off it and onto the soggy field, trying to see into the shed. As he crept past a thick hedge, it moved.

Kyle jumped out, knocking into the officer, throwing him off-balance. He tussled with him on the ground while the other partner ran forward, shouting, "FREEZE!"

But Kyle was running now, sprinting across the field, through a row of bushes, and into a parking lot. The younger officer took pursuit, but he was loaded down with equipment and was no match for Kyle.

Kirsten watched Kyle disappear over the hill and out of sight. Then she went over to the older officer, who was drenched from his fall onto the waterlogged turf. "Are you okay?" he asked. Then he reached down to his holster. "Son of a bitch. He took my pistol."

CRACCCCK!

Kirsten flinched at the sound just over the hill. It was a gunshot. Kirsten had never heard one before, but it sounded like fireworks—that's how people always describe it—and it could have been Kyle's gun or the cop's, but *someone* had been shot at.

From the officer's belt, a walkie-talkie squawked, "Request backup!" He took off in a run, and Kirsten followed.

They crossed the road, approaching the crest of a hill, and Kirsten braced herself, wondering if Sam's murderer was now dead.

The young officer, who was trudging toward them, looked shaken. "No one was hurt," he said. "I thought the guy didn't have a gun."

"He took mine," the other man said.

The younger cop looked toward the east edge of the park, and Kirsten followed his glance over the stone gate, into the ribbons of light along Fifth Avenue, and along the amber rectangles of apartments coming to life with preparations for dinner. And she knew that, somewhere, Kyle was running hard, making plans to escape again and to lie low, wrapped in a fantasy of lies that, this time, she hoped would come crashing around him. She would make sure she did whatever she could to make that happen.

"Motherfucker," the young cop said, staring off into the distance.

Kirsten smiled a weary smile. *"Le débauché de la mère."*

"Huh?"

"Never mind," she replied. "It's a Woodley joke."

EPILOGUE

"**I would put vitamin** E on those suckers," Scott the bartender said as he examined Kirsten's wrists in the dim light over the Party Room bar.

After two days, her wrists were still red from the tape. It had been good for plenty of attention at school, but Kirsten didn't really want that. Sam's and Emma's deaths still hung heavily over everyone, but Kirsten's story had been, in its own way, a bright light—a life saved, a culprit discovered.

She'd been interviewed on-air four times, shown her wrists to a nationwide audience. She'd even gotten Brandon to give his picture of Kyle to the media, and it was televised, too, enhanced for clarity.

Over the last twenty-four hours, other photos of Kyle had surfaced, from his friend at Columbia and from old Talcott schoolmates.

They all claimed that Kyle was a nice guy, and that it was unimaginable he'd do this.

The two police officers, Percy Charles Randolph (the younger one) and Walter Schmidt (the older), had become heroes, the theft of Schmidt's gun conveniently not mentioned in the news reports—though Percy had found it in the park right where Kyle had dropped it, where it had accidentally discharged a round.

Kirsten's parents had taken her out to a subdued candlelight dinner last night, the celebration of gratitude for Kirsten's life tempered by prayers for Sam and Emma.

It was Kirsten's idea to spend tonight at the Party Room with Julie, Carla, and Sarah. There had been more tears than laughs tonight, and Kirsten had heard a million times how relieved everyone was that she'd been spared.

Kirsten appreciated that, but at night, when she had to fall asleep, she couldn't help wondering what it had been like for Sam and Emma the nights they'd died and how they must have felt when they'd known they wouldn't escape.

That was the hardest thing of all, and she didn't know if she'd ever get over it.

Julie danced over, looking gorgeous in her new Stella McCartney number, and of course bringing along a crowd of guys. "Aren't you going to dance?" she asked.

"Later," Kirsten said.

They'd talked it over before, she and Julie. The days had been so full of tears, and it was important to honor Sam's *and* Emma's spirit by living life, by doing the things they loved to do so much.

But it wasn't easy.

Bleeeep.

The bar phone rang, and Scott snatched it up. "Party Room, Scott speaking . . ."

Kirsten turned and watched the action on the floor. The Woodley lacrosse team had arrived, and by the looks of their dance moves, they still thought they were out on the field.

"*Who?*" Scott was nearly shouting to be heard over the racket. "Yeah, you bet she is . . ." He held out the phone to Kirsten. "You're the popular one tonight!"

Kirsten pressed the phone to her ear, covering her other ear against the noise. "Hello? *Hello?*"

She heard a voice at the other end, but it was only a mumble. The lacrosse guys were blotting out even the dance music. She hopped off her stool and crossed behind the bar to the hallway that led to the bathrooms. It was a little quieter there. "Sorry. Try again—and speak louder!" She pressed the phone closer to her ear.

This time she heard the words clearly.

"It's me," the voice said. Kyle's voice. "It isn't supposed to be like this. We'll see each other again. I'm coming back as soon as I can."

Her fingers went slack. She let the phone fall.

But Kyle had already hung up.

THE PARTY CONTINUES!

Don't miss the next book in the Party Room trilogy, *After Hours*, by Morgan Burke.

As Kirsten unfolded another paper, she remembered how Sam had broken up with Brandon and how badly he had taken it. And how terrible Brandon had looked just a few nights ago. Then she read the note:

> Brando—I saw Jones again. I had to.
> I know you'll be angry w/ me, but I had to.
> I have to keep seeing him. I just have to.

Kirsten furrowed her brows. *Sam never mentioned any Jones guy to* me. She rushed through the rest of the note. She couldn't believe what she was reading. Apparently Sam was seeing this Jones guy on the side. And Brandon knew about it! *How come Sam never said anything about it?*

She scanned the next note:

> I can't go on like this. It's got to stop,
> Brandon. Don't go to Volume again, please.
> I'm telling you for your own good. Stay away
> from Jones. He's really pissed and I don't

think I can control the situation anymore. It's
major. Trust me, this isn't like at Talcott, B.
Just do me a favor and keep your butt OUT
of VOLUME!!! Okay?

Kirsten read the last two notes again.
Although the scraps of information that
Kirsten could pick out were sketchy at best,
she felt as if she was seeing a whole new chapter of Sam's life. Kirsten had never heard of
this Jones guy. Volume? Was it a bar? Kirsten
had never been there.

Kirsten wondered if this had something to
do with why Sam broke up with Brandon.
Now that Kirsten thought about it, Sam had
never actually said why she dumped him.
What did she mean—"This is major"?

She couldn't make out the story, but something was going on between her and Brandon
right up to the day Sam broke up with him
and maybe the night she disappeared!

Who is Jones? Why didn't Sam tell her
about him?

The warm feelings of nostalgia drained out
of Kirsten as she realized that her best friend,
her *sister* practically, had kept a secret from
her. By the looks of it, an *enormous* secret.

feel the fear.

FEAR STREET® NIGHTS

A brand-new Fear Street trilogy by the master of horror

R.L. STINE

Coming in Summer 2005

Simon Pulse
Published by Simon & Schuster
Fear Street is a registered trademark of Parachute Press, Inc.

NEWLY WED

Nancy Krulik

The honeymoon just ended.
And Jesse and Jen are about to
get a hilarious helping of reality.

It's a year in the life of one young couple, two
opinionated best friends, and more meddling
family members than you can count.

This I swear.

PUBLISHED BY SIMON PULSE

Jeremy Iversen

21 The age at which freedom rings
    The number of drinks consumed in one night

The honest new novel about the
greatest day in a college kid's life

PUBLISHED BY SIMON PULSE

As many as 1 in 3 Americans
who have HIV... don't know it.

TAKE CONTROL.
KNOW YOUR STATUS.
GET TESTED.

To learn more about HIV testing,
or get a free guide to HIV and
other sexually transmitted diseases:

**www.knowhivaids.org
1-866-344-KNOW**

Check Your **PULSE** Book Club

Sign up for the CHECK YOUR PULSE
free teen e-mail book club!

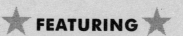 ★ **FEATURING** ★

A new book discussion every month

Monthly book giveaways

Chapter excerpts

Book discussions with the authors

Literary horoscopes

Plus YOUR comments!

To sign up go to www.SimonSaysTEEN.com
don't forget to CHECK YOUR PULSE!